Kara

SpringSong ❧ Books

Kara

Lisa

Michelle

SpringSong & Books

Kara

Carole Gift Page

BETHANY HOUSE PUBLISHERS
MINNEAPOLIS, MINNESOTA 55438

Kara
Carole Gift Page

Library of Congress Catalog Card Number 93–74534

ISBN 1–55661–448–9

Published by Bethany House Publishers
A Ministry of Bethany Fellowship, Inc.
11300 Hampshire Avenue South
Minneapolis, Minnesota 55438

Printed in the United States of America

To David and Lisa

and their

precious little

Lauren

CAROLE GIFT PAGE is an award-winning author, writing instructor, and conference speaker who has written over thirty books and has published over eight hundred stories, articles, and poems. She and her husband co-founded the Inland Empire Christian Writer's Guild, and Carole is currently the fiction columnist for *The Christian Communicator*. The parents of three children, Carole and her husband make their home in Moreno Valley, California.

1

$\mathcal{B}$en Strickland died for no reason. Kara knew she would never understand it. Even when she replayed the details in her mind, organizing the facts like items arranged precisely in a newspaper article, she was stunned afresh by the suddenness of her father's death. It couldn't have happened. But it did. The facts were sure, indisputable.

On the first day of spring that year, late in the evening of March twentieth, the handsome Dr. Ben Strickland unexpectedly walked out of his sprawling, two-story colonial home in the elite residential section of Westchester, climbed into his red LeBaron convertible, and sped off into the night.

The state patrol arrived several hours later to inform Anna Strickland that her husband had died upon impact when his vehicle plunged into a nearby ravine. In shock, Anna repeated over and over that she could not imagine why he had gone out. To her knowledge he had not been summoned to the hospital to see a patient. When the officers asked if he had been drinking or whether he could have been emotionally upset, Anna began weeping hysterically and finally had to be sedated.

Kara, asleep upstairs, had no knowledge of the grim events transpiring that evening. Startled into wakefulness by her mother's agonized cries, Kara stumbled downstairs, bleary-eyed, her mind still steeped in dreams, only to stand dumbstruck with horror as the policeman relayed his grisly news.

Kara could only murmur through her tears that just hours ago she had kissed him good-night. No, she wouldn't believe it. The officers had to be mistaken. Surely her father was just asleep upstairs. He had no reason to be out at this time of night, she argued.

But her protests were in vain. Mere words, meaningless denials. There was no mistake. He was dead. It was final and irrevocable.

Kara Strickland cried herself to sleep every night that spring, but after that first terrible night, her mother refused to cry. Instead, Anna became bitter and withdrawn, her eyes like nails—cold, hard, tearless. She kept a bottle of vodka by her bedside and smoked four packs of cigarettes a day. She never mentioned her husband's death, and she never bothered to pack up his things or acknowledge his absence. Ben Strickland remained an invisible presence in the huge old house that had been his for nearly twenty years.

While Anna sought to dissolve her grief in alcohol, Kara suffered through her own emotional upheavals. In the May first entry of her diary, she wrote:

> Since my father died, a great deal of what I am has ceased to exist. There are things about me only he knew, things I never told my mother. He took the real me with him to the grave—the "me" whom only he had taken time to find. No one else really knows me. They are only acquainted with the shell I live in—plain, brash, impulsive. They don't really know who lives inside. But my father did. And he is gone. If someone cried, *Will the real Kara Strickland please stand up,* I would have to say, "She is not here. She is buried with her father's memories." Listen, I am disgustingly morbid. I have never been especially fond of myself. Perhaps there is something in me to love—my father loved me—but I am not certain what that something is. Or

whether it is there at all. Scary, thinking that. Daddy, why did you have to go away?

In her grief, Kara discovered a companion of sorts. Peter Bremer, a lanky, sandy-haired guy with pale green eyes and legs like poles, attended Summit High and had been her class-mate since grade school. Out of politeness, or perhaps from genuine sympathy, he attended Ben Strickland's funeral. Af-terward he called on Kara, took her out from time to time, and patiently endured her shifting moods. His own father had died two years before, so he knew how it felt to lose someone close. He was ready for Kara's occasional fits of anger and her frequent bouts with depression.

At first Kara's grief pierced too deep to allow her to de-velop a serious interest in Peter. Yet she leaned on him, de-pending on his emotional support. There was no one else. Certainly not her mother. Not now. Peter provided a diver-sion, offering sweet relief to the deadness that pervaded her house and her heart.

As the weeks passed, Peter spent an increasing amount of time at the Strickland house, he and Kara sharing hours of homework and TV, devouring colas and mushroom pizzas, listening to their favorite music, and speculating over what each would do following graduation in June.

However, not once during those two months did Peter touch Kara, not even attempting so much as a good-night kiss. At times Kara fretted over this. She was aware that she was not particularly attractive. She was perhaps too tall and too thin; her long, straight brown hair with auburn highlights was in her opinion plain and boring. Her only redeeming fea-ture was her eyes—large, thickly lashed, a rich mahogany brown. But were eyes enough?

Kara, eighteen in April, had had few dates and was, she suspected, less experienced with the opposite sex than some fifteen-year-olds she knew. She wondered if Peter merely cared for her as a friend. Did he leave her alone because he sensed her awkwardness and uncertainty? Or was it out of respect for her grief? Then again, maybe he simply was not interested in pursuing a physical relationship.

These nagging questions were answered one evening early in June while Kara and Peter sat together on the sofa in her living room, cramming for final exams. It was late. Anna had already gone upstairs to bed. Peter looked exhausted. He was in the process of listing the advantages and disadvantages of the American two-party political system when suddenly he put his arms around Kara and kissed her soundly. She felt herself stiffen momentarily, then surprisingly, wonderfully, she relaxed. When Peter released her, she wanted to tell him not to stop.

"I've been thinking about doing that for a long time," he said. "I like you a lot, Kara."

"I like you too," she murmured, and he kissed her again. After that their studies were forgotten. Kara sat nestled in the crook of Peter's arm, her head resting against his cheek. For the first time since her father's death she felt alive. Sensing that these moments with Peter were precious and fleeting, she yearned to hold on to them, never to let them die.

Then she thought of her mother. "You'd better go, Peter," she whispered. "If Anna knew you were still here, she'd have a fit."

Peter stirred reluctantly. "Yeah, yeah. I get the message. We've had enough for one night."

Flustered, Kara said, "That's not it. I—I like kissing you, being close—"

"You haven't done much of that, have you?" said Peter offhandedly, standing up and stretching.

Kara stood up too and shook her head.

"How come?"

She shrugged. "Anna never lets me date much. She always says I shouldn't get involved with guys until I'm out of

school. Crazy, huh? I guess there haven't been many oppor-
tunities anyway."

"What does she think of me?" he asked, his voice deliberately casual.

"She thinks you're okay. As long as we're just friends."

Peter pulled her into his arms. "I hate to tell you this,
but your mother is warped." With a playful chuckle he sought
her mouth. Instinctively Kara drew back.

"You've got to go, Peter. Anna—"

"Oh, Anna this, Anna that," he chided. "Why do you
call her Anna, anyway? She's your mother, isn't she?"

"Of course," Kara laughed uncomfortably. "I've just always called her Anna. I don't know why."

Peter led her back to the couch and sat her down. "One
for the road and I'll go." He kissed her hard, more insistently
than before, and Kara found herself caught between the desire to hold him closer and the sudden fear that he might not
let her go. In that delicious instant of swaying between the
tenuous poles of passion and reason, Kara heard the shrill,
screaming voice of her mother.

"Let go of her! Get out! Do you hear? Get out of this
house!"

Startled, Peter jumped to his feet, slapped his papers and
books together, and dashed to the door, slamming it behind
him before Kara could comprehend what was happening. She
stared dumbly at her mother, silenced momentarily by the
woman's rage.

Anna, an intense, thin-faced woman, stood wrapped in a
burgundy terry cloth bathrobe, hands on her hips, her un-
combed frosted brown hair sprouting from her head in odd
little twiglike tufts. She nailed Kara to the wall with her gaze,
"The minute I let you out of my sight you act like a tramp,"
she hissed, her words slurred and her eyes bloodshot.

"You've been drinking, Anna," said Kara coldly. "Go
back to bed."

Her mother stepped forward, stumbled, caught herself, and slumped down into a chair. "Where are my cigarettes?" she whined, probing her bathrobe pockets. "Where did Ben hide my cigarettes?"

Kara went over behind her mother's chair and began to massage the back of her neck. "You probably left them upstairs," she chided, as though answering a child.

Anna reached up, caught Kara's hand, and held it fast. "Don't let that boy come back. Promise me he won't come back here."

Kara flinched. "I can't, Anna. I like Peter. He likes me. You can't make me stay a little girl forever."

Anna squeezed Kara's hand until she winced. The older woman's voice was almost a sob. "Please be a good girl. Don't be like your mother."

Kara gently retrieved her hand. "Don't talk like that," she scolded, forcing a small, puzzled laugh. "Why shouldn't I be like you? You're not so bad, are you?"

Her mother ignored her feeble attempt at humor. "I can never reach you. Only Ben. He should be here. You'd listen to him."

Kara helped Anna back to bed, taking care to remove the half-empty vodka bottle from the nightstand. She poured the contents down the bathroom drain, then dropped the empty bottle into the wastebasket.

In her own room, Kara felt a profound sadness wash away the remnants of pleasure lingering from her moments in Peter's arms. Why couldn't she still feel his closeness? Why did she feel even lonelier now? Did Peter only remind her of her father's unwavering devotion?

Heavy questions. She was overreacting, being ridiculously emotional. Kara knew that. She had to block out such thoughts, preserve her sanity. Sleep. Somehow she needed to force her mind into oblivion. She fought for it, lost, wrestled more determinedly against sleeplessness, and lost again. Toward morning she succumbed to exhaustion. When the alarm jangled a couple of hours later, she bolted upright, breathless, her heart pounding furiously. She was as tired now as she had been the night before.

Having dressed in her most comfortable jeans and a sweatshirt, she brushed her cheeks with a hint of color and ran a comb quickly through long auburn hair. Kara speculated on her situation and arrived at certain basic conclusions. She was, for all practical purposes, an adult. Yet she wasn't exactly sure who she was supposed to be, nor why it really mattered that she find out. In a few days she would graduate from high school. But what would she do then? Most of her classmates were looking forward to college, a job, or marriage. Kara peered into her own nebulous future. As far as she was concerned there was nothing. Neither did she desire anything in particular—except that she might have a purpose worth striving for and someone who cared.

Her father had cared, but he was gone. Her mother— well, somehow Anna had always remained at the periphery of Kara's life, fretting over this or that, but seldom participating in Kara's concerns the way her father had. Whenever her father was free from his heavy schedule at the hospital, he and Kara would spend hours together in his study going over the articles and editorials she had written for the school paper. Or they would take leisurely walks at twilight while he shared little anecdotes about his patients or colleagues, or expressed enthusiasm over some new medical procedure. Their friendship was sweet, natural, spontaneous. With her father, she had never needed to question who she was or where she was going. She wondered momentarily whether it was truly her mother's strict rules that had kept her from dating, or could it also have been her unswerving devotion to her father?

Did it really matter now? Her father was dead, cut out of her life in one incisive blow. She would never recover. She perceived this fact and accepted it. Like someone with a physical handicap, she would manage somehow. She would survive, but she would never be the same.

With a twinge of regret, Kara understood that her mother would not be the same either. Although her parents had never been especially close, Kara recognized that Anna, too, had been devastated by her husband's death. That had to be the reason she had turned herself into an alcoholic, drinking day and night. That was why she smoked incessantly now, one cigarette after another, puffing nervously, impatiently, until each white tobacco-filled stem was reduced to ashes. Kara wondered how much longer Anna's nerves would hold up before she exploded—or collapsed.

But she would not think of that now either, for there was nothing she could do. She would concentrate only on good things. Like Peter. Perhaps he held the secret to Kara's future. Maybe someday she could grow to love him enough to devote her life to him as she had to her father. Why not? What else did she have now, if not Peter?

Dwelling on such possibilities, Kara headed downstairs for breakfast. Anna was not up yet. Naturally. Without enthusiasm Kara poured herself a glass of orange juice and reached for the milk and cornflakes. It was no fun eating alone.

Before leaving for school, Kara slipped into her father's study. Each morning she came here and stood in the quiet among his things—his desk, his chair, his papers stacked in neat piles. His medical library with a few cherished mementos in the bookcase—crude clay creatures Kara had molded for him in grade school, souvenirs from long-forgotten vacations, trinkets and gifts from Christmases past. In this room Kara felt close to her father, as if at any moment he might enter and take his place among his treasures.

It was a bittersweet fantasy that Kara embroidered upon each time she entered the study. The place was magical, open to vast impossibilities. She loved her father's books, savored touching them, browsing through them. Even the pictures on the walls seemed special—the recent studio photograph of Kara for her high school graduation, her parents' quaint, slightly faded wedding picture with her mother, small and smiling, beside her tall, squinting, serious-looking father. And of course, there was the old black-and-white snapshot of Aunt Catherine, her mother's sister, whom the family rarely saw. Indeed, her father's collection of photographs contributed their own nostalgic warmth to the room. It was good. She felt better somehow. Now she could go out and face the world—at least today.

2

*K*ara could not read the silent, expressionless woman who sat across from her at the dinner table that evening. Anna was frequently preoccupied during meals but seemed even quieter than usual, scarcely touching her food. Was her mother feeling remorse over her drunken outburst the night before? Or was she sulking because she understood at last that she could not control her daughter's life? Or had she slipped into an even deeper depression over her husband's death?

Kara wondered for an instant why she even tried to understand her mother. Then, chagrined, she made an attempt at conversation.

"I think I did well on my English final," she offered with forced enthusiasm. "We had to write an essay on a major social issue, and you know how I love to write. I wrote on abortion."

Anna looked up, apparently interested. "Why did you write on that—on abortion?"

Kara shrugged. "I don't know. Maybe because a girl in my class had an abortion and she seemed proud of it, actually proud. She disgusted me. I think she should have kept her baby. How could she destroy it without a thought?"

Anna picked gingerly at the noodles on her plate. Her expression shifted several times, so subtly that Kara felt baffled. "A girl gets into trouble," remarked Anna in a peculiar monotone. "She panics . . . she knows she's trapped. She's

16

liable to do anything. A girl has to be careful that nothing like that ever happens."

Now Kara understood. Anna was clearly referring to her and Peter. "Well, if you're worried about Peter and me—" she began defensively.

"He's not for you," Anna interrupted firmly. "You think he'll take your father's place, but he won't. No one ever will, not for either of us."

A lump swelled in Kara's throat, and she realized she was no longer hungry. She pushed back her chair and stood up, recognizing with despair the truth of her mother's words. Indeed, who could ever take Ben Strickland's place in their lives?

"I have one more final to study for, so I'd better get busy," said Kara, excusing herself and leaving the room. From the corner of her eye she caught a glimpse of her mother, still faintly attractive, moving intently toward the liquor cabinet.

Kara couldn't sleep any better than she had the night before. Her hours of study had proved fruitless; she could recall little of the material. In the early predawn shadows, Kara felt more vulnerable and lonely than ever. Even her father's house offered her no comfort now. During these eerie nocturnal hours it seemed that she and her mother were entombed in these walls with her father's ghost. She was tempted to rise and flee to his study, where memories always flowed with warmth and joy. But she feared to go there tonight lest even that precious sanctuary be tainted by the gloom surrounding her.

At last she slept. Not well, though, for dreams slipped in, obscure and frightening. She struggled against them, trying to alter their outcome, but she only exhausted herself. She stirred, pushed at her covers, sleepily aware of a stuffiness in the room, a lack of air. She woke reluctantly and nudged her groggy mind through a cobweb of dreams. Forcing her body to function, she sat up, conscious of a change in the atmosphere. A dimness nearly overshadowing the dark. Stifling! And there were sounds. A persistent scratching on the walls. A muted popping noise somewhere beyond her room.

For an instant Kara thought of burglars. Then she smelled smoke and recognized the crackling sounds. Fire! She leaped from her bed, grabbed the telephone from the nightstand, and with trembling fingers dialed 911. She fought back her rising panic as she reported her message. Then, dropping the phone, she bounded out of her room and into the smoke-filled hallway.

She raced to her mother's door and groped desperately for the knob. Her fingers, touching hot metal, drew back in pain. A debilitating horror converged on Kara's mind as she understood that the fire originated in Anna's room. She stood momentarily paralyzed. Then, swiftly she wrapped a corner of her cotton nightgown around the knob and struggled to turn it. Seconds passed intolerably. At last the door opened, revealing a thick wall of smoke. The heat stunned her. She coughed and turned away, covering her mouth and nose with her gown.

She would never be able to penetrate that blanket of deadly fumes. Frantically she ran back to her bedroom and peered through the shadows in an agonizing instant of indecision. Then, with a surprising surge of energy, she pulled the sheet from her bed, raced to the adjoining bathroom, and turned on the tub faucet full blast. She soaked the sheet thoroughly, then dragged it into the hallway toward her mother's room.

A wall of flames confronted her.

"Oh, dear God, no!"

Kara drew back from the heat, dazed. The flames were

blinding, a macabre dance of dazzling, ethereal shapes and colors. She screamed for Anna.

Pulling the heavy, water-soaked sheet over her like a shroud, Kara knelt down and crawled on her knees through the leapfrogging flames toward Anna's bed. She held her breath, remembering that the poisonous gases could kill as quickly as the flames. The incredible heat sapped her strength, turned her arms and legs to putty. Sheer determination propelled Kara inch by inch along the floor. Was she moving in the right direction? Would the fumes overcome her?

Before she reached the bed, she found her mother's body crumpled on the floor. "Anna!" she rasped, but the dry ache in her throat squelched her voice. Swiftly Kara enveloped her mother with her in the sheet and dragged the dead weight of Anna's body along the floor.

It was an appalling journey, painstakingly slow. Kara, nearly overwhelmed by her gigantic task, longed to surrender to the inviting drowsiness that pressed upon her.

No. Go on. Inch by precious inch. Find the door. Oh, God, where is it! Please don't let us die!

Through the door at last. Was Anna alive? Her body did not respond. Kara could hardly move now. The vile smoke had curled inside her nostrils and scorched the membranes of her throat. Fits of coughing seized her, tearing painfully through her throat and chest. It occurred to her that the heat might burst her lungs, the smoke snuff out her senses.

Kara groped blindly along the carpeted floor for the stairway. Unless she got Anna downstairs there would be no hope of survival. Her hands searched furiously. *Yes. There!* The stairs. An unexpected reserve of strength awakened her weary muscles, providing a brief impetus for the support of her unconscious charge.

Down the stairs. Step by step. The weight of her mother's body nearly staggering, pushing her down. Kara realized that there was no way she could make it down the stairs. Involuntarily she gasped for air. Only excruciating pain rewarded her frantic effort to breathe.

Halfway down Kara collapsed. Imprisoned by Anna's weight, she succumbed gratefully to warmth and sleep, blotting out the agonies of pain and exhaustion.

3

$\mathcal{K}$ara was a child again, running, skipping over a grassy hillside. Emerald green. A cerulean sky. She ran into the arms of her father, Dr. Ben Strickland, the prominent Westchester surgeon, a wise and gentle man. He raised her into the air, tossing her deftly, catching her with ease, tossing her again, his laughter ringing with hers, an extraordinary melody. He tossed her again—up, up, away. This time she remained suspended, light as air, a vacuous presence in the boundless heavens. There were no arms to catch her. No laughter. She would float unhampered, unobserved, forever . . .

A room began to take shape. Walls appeared, hazy, hastily formed. There was nothing solid yet, but something. A definite structure; and objects. A dresser. A bed. The form of someone nearby.

Kara's eyes focused finally. Yes, she could see. There was a window on the opposite wall with dark blue curtains. A man stood between her and the window. He seemed to be waiting patiently, his arms folded in a gesture of calm solemnity. *Daddy?*

Kara tried to move. She couldn't. She realized now that she was in bed. A sheet covered her body, and her arms were wrapped in bandages. In her mind she asked, *Where am I?* But she was too weary to form the words with her lips. She already knew the answer.

As though she had asked the question out loud, the

white-clad man stepped forward and said pleasantly, "You're in the hospital, Kara. You were brought in yesterday morning. But don't worry. You're going to be just fine."

Kara forced the words from her mouth. "Who—are you?" The man smiled affably. "I'm Dr. Kasdorf. We've met before, but you were quite a bit younger. In fact, so was I!" His face shifted into an expression of sober recollection. "I was a colleague of your father's. He was a great man and one of the best surgeons in the state."

Kara attempted to nod, but to her dismay she found any movement painful.

Dr. Kasdorf approached her bed. "It'll be that way for a few more days—the pain, I mean," he told her, his voice low and confidential. "But you're a fortunate young lady. It could have been much worse."

"How bad—?" Kara formed the words laboriously.

"You have first- and second-degree burns on your hands and arms, you're suffering from some smoke inhalation, and your hair was singed a bit. But shortly you'll be as good as new," he said. "I've been in touch with Dr. Lasky, your family physician, and he'll check in on you this afternoon."

Kara strained forward slightly, suddenly intent. "Anna?"

"Your mother?" said Dr. Kasdorf, his expression adjusting guardedly. "I was with her earlier. Dr. Lasky is with her now. I think I'll let him give you a report. You can be sure she's getting the best of care."

Kara lay back, releasing the tension in her muscles, and closed her eyes. Memories of the fire were beginning to invade her mind. She could picture herself—seemingly outside her body and watching in a state of blank terror—as she, Kara Strickland, coped with a burning house. To her eternal frustration it seemed that she moved in slow motion, the way one runs, yet scarcely advances, while being pursued by grisly phantoms in a nightmare. No gesture, no impulse was quick enough. The moments appeared to stretch into an eternity, yet eternity remained dwarfed by the moment. It was a nightmare, and she had lived through it.

Now a dozen questions prodded her thoughts, but she had no strength to ask them. Instead, her mind focused on the pain surging through her extremities. She managed to ask, "If the burns . . . aren't bad, why do they hurt so much?"

Dr. Kasdorf's words were precise, reasonable. "Because the nerve endings are exposed and sensitive. The bandages will keep out the air, and you'll be receiving medication periodically. I assure you, we'll be watching you closely, young lady. Now I think you should get some rest." He turned to go, then paused reflectively. "You were wise to protect yourself with the water-soaked sheet, Miss Strickland. It may very well have saved your life."

That afternoon, Dr. Lasky, a middle-aged man with gray-black hair and a dry, puckered expression, appeared by Kara's bedside. Not an attractive man, he had puffy lips, a bulbous, slightly crooked nose, and eyes seemingly imbedded in small pouches of flesh. But the doctor, a wise, kindly, soft-spoken man, had been her father's closest friend and their family physician for as long as Kara could remember.

Kara, who had been dozing, was startled by Dr. Lasky's presence. But immediately she felt comforted to have him beside her. Without warning, tears welled up in her eyes. "Dr. Lasky—" she began.

"Yes, my child, I know," he said sympathetically. "You've had quite an experience."

"How is Anna?" she murmured.

Dr. Lasky's face betrayed concern in spite of his effort to be reassuring. "Your mother—she had quite a time of it, dear. She's in the burn ward, receiving the best possible care. You know our hospital has one of the best burn units in the state."

"Then she'll be all right?" persisted Kara.

He made a slight coughing sound in his throat. "There are no guarantees—"

"I don't want guarantees, Dr. Lasky. I just want the truth. Please, tell me how she is."

Dr. Lasky pulled a chair over beside Kara's bed and sat down. His expression was sober, his voice quiet and controlled. "I won't try to fool you, Kara. Your mother is lucky to be alive. She inhaled toxic fumes and received third-degree burns on over thirty percent of her body. But we're doing everything we can for her."

"She won't die, will she?" said Kara, hardly daring to ask.

Dr. Lasky's lips twisted into a slight, unconvincing smile. "Let's not look at the negative side of things, Kara. Let's just concentrate on the positive, shall we?"

Kara nodded obediently, but she mildly resented Dr. Lasky's double-talk. She knew how patients could be kept in the dark about their true conditions. But it would do little good to push Dr. Lasky now. She realized that he considered himself a surrogate father and would do whatever was necessary to protect his young charge.

Dr. Lasky stood up and glanced at his watch. "Before I go, Kara, is there anything I can do for you? Anyone you want me to contact?"

Kara considered this. "There is someone. A boy at school."

Dr. Lasky smiled. "You wouldn't be speaking of Peter Bremer, would you?"

"Yes. How—?" Kara felt her face flush.

"He's outside. Been waiting nearly an hour to see you. I told him he could come in for a few minutes as soon as I was through." Dr. Lasky took a step toward the door, then hesitated and threw Kara a strange, quizzical glance. "Your mother has a sister, doesn't she? Shouldn't she be notified?"

Kara felt an inexplicable sinking sensation in her chest. "Yes, Anna has one sister," she said dully. "She lives in the southern part of the state. But she's never been close to us.

She didn't even attend my father's funeral."

Dr. Lasky rubbed his chin thoughtfully, methodically. "Just the same, I'd like to contact her. You and Anna will both be needing her help now."

"Why do we need her?" argued Kara dryly. "Dr. Kasdorf said I'll be all right soon. Then I can take care of Anna myself."

"No, I'm afraid not," replied Dr. Lasky, shaking his head gravely. "You may be released from the hospital in a matter of days, Kara, but only if you have someone to watch over you for a few weeks. As for your mother, you're familiar with the procedures of burn therapy and the necessary skin-graft operations. You must realize that Anna has a long road ahead of her."

Kara nodded reluctantly. She didn't want to hear this. All she wanted to do was turn back the clock, to escape back to the privacy and security she and Anna had shared in Ben Strickland's house. Why did fate seem determined to destroy everything—and everyone—she cared about?

"When can I see Anna?" she asked.

"Not for a few days yet. The danger of infection is too great," Dr. Lasky told her. "But don't fret now. You'll be the first to hear when she can have visitors. Besides, you need rest and quiet yourself."

The doctor went to the door and beckoned outside, then glanced back at Kara. "Here's your Mr. Bremer. Don't let him stay too long."

Peter stepped inside but stood formally by the door, his eyes carefully avoiding Kara's.

"Go on in, Peter," Dr. Lasky cajoled lightly. "You'll be good medicine for her." He addressed Kara more seriously. "What did you say your aunt's name is?"

"I didn't say."

"Your stubbornness is showing, Kara, my girl."

"Catherine," she responded, giving in with a slight pout. "Catherine Hardin."

"And she lives in—"

"Claremont."

Dr. Lasky smiled congenially. "Thank you for cooperating, Kara. I'll get in touch with her tonight."

"It won't do any good," warned Kara sarcastically. "She won't come."

Dr. Lasky left without acknowledging Kara's bitter prediction. The room seemed suddenly empty, too silent, too large. Peter remained by the door. Kara wondered if he might turn and run out. She tried to remember the last time they had been together. Peter had held her and kissed her. Now he looked as if he would like to flee. Was she that repulsive?

"Peter—"

"Hello, Kara." He moved toward her slowly, his long arms dangling awkwardly at his sides. "Kara, I'm so sorry. I—"

"How did you find out?"

"The radio. They told all about the fire on the news. I couldn't believe it. I should have known your mother would do something like this."

Kara flinched. "What do you mean?"

Peter waved his hand nervously. "Oh, I shouldn't say anything, I guess. The doctors would have my scalp. But I can't help it. That woman almost killed you."

"What are you talking about?" demanded Kara.

"Your mother," replied Peter angrily. "Didn't you know? She was drunk. She fell asleep with a lighted cigarette. The firemen reported that the fire probably smoldered for hours in her mattress."

Kara felt momentarily dazed. She hadn't thought to ask how the fire started. So it had been Anna—her vodka, her incessant smoking, her terrible depression. She had done this to them. The pain in Kara's arms intensified with this new pain of comprehension. She wanted to cry out, but didn't.

"I don't want to talk about it, Peter," she told him flatly.

"Sure, I understand."

"I must look terrible," she said uneasily, wishing she could move her arms and touch her face. She hadn't seen herself in a mirror yet. The thought spurred an unaccustomed panic that nearly snatched her breath away.

"It's not that bad," observed Peter. "You're lucky your face wasn't burned. Dr. Lasky said you're going to be all right."

"I missed my algebra final," she remarked.

Peter nodded. "I stopped by Mrs. Corby's room and explained why you weren't there. She was awfully sorry. She said your grades are good enough that she'll waive the exam so you can still graduate with the class."

"Thank you for seeing her, Peter. Mrs. Corby's a neat lady. But, Peter, graduation—!" Kara's face darkened and she moaned audibly. "Graduation is this weekend, Peter. I won't be able to attend the prom or the ceremonies or anything!"

Peter looked appropriately sympathetic. "It's a rotten deal, Kara. No one should have to miss their graduation."

Kara laid her head back on the pillow and closed her eyes. "I won't be able to go with you to the prom, Peter."

"Yeah, I know," he replied unevenly.

"You'll have to go with someone else," she said.

"I hate to do that, Kara."

"You must. There's no sense in both of us missing the prom."

There was silence for a moment. Then Peter conceded, "I guess you're right, Kara. It *is* the biggest event of the year."

"Then you'll go?"

Peter cleared his throat. "I was sort of thinking of asking Jenny Patterson. I mean, I shouldn't just go by myself, not to something like the prom. Not that Jenny's anything special, of course—"

"Yes, I know Jenny." Kara could not bring herself to open her eyes or gaze into Peter's face.

"You're sure you wouldn't be mad if I asked her?" he persisted.

"No," said Kara. She fought to hold back the tears forming under her eyelids. "I'm awfully tired, Peter. I should try to sleep. You understand, don't you?"

"Oh, sure, sure, Kara," he replied, scarcely disguising his relief. "I'll stop in again real soon. You just take care of yourself and get well, okay?"

Kara did not open her eyes until after Peter had gone. Only then did the swelling layer of tears spill out freely, making tiny rivulets down her cheeks and running into her ears. The tears came faster as Kara realized in hot frustration that neither hand was free to wipe them away.

Peter would never stop in again. She knew that with a terrible certainty. At this moment her life seemed even more at an end than the day her father died!

4

*L*ate the next afternoon, a tall, slender woman entered Kara's room, her graceful figure stylishly accented by a sleek forest green dress, with matching high heels and purse. She gazed at Kara with inscrutable, deep brown eyes, pain-filled, compassionate.

Kara said coldly, "Hello, Aunt Kate," and looked away.

"May I come in?" Catherine Hardin took a tentative step forward.

"Whatever you wish," said Kara.

The woman seemed immediately out of place in the hospital setting. Kara was grudgingly aware of her aunt's quiet, self-contained gentility, her finely carved features, and her smooth, precise gestures. Kara had always thought of her aunt as an impeccable woman, though she did not use the term kindly. Impeccable suggested rigid perfection, a lack of forbearance and affinity with the rest of flawed humanity. Why else had Aunt Kate kept her distance from the family for so many years?

"I was so sorry to hear about the accident," said Catherine in her softly melodic voice, her narrow brows arching slightly. She put out a hand to touch Kara's bandaged arm, then apparently thought better of the idea. "Oh, Kara," she said, her voice filling with a startling agony. Her perfect face looked momentarily as if it might shatter.

"I'm okay," Kara said unthinkingly. A ridiculous statement, of course, when she probably resembled a mummy.

29

"I came as soon as I could," continued Catherine. "When Dr. Lasky called me, I was shocked. I couldn't imagine such a tragedy happening so soon after your father's death."

For a moment Kara dropped her defenses and looked searchingly at her aunt. "Have you seen Anna yet? How is she?"

"No, I haven't seen her. I came here first. The nurse at the desk said I'd have to get the doctor's permission to see her. They're apparently concerned about infection."

"She has to be all right," said Kara solemnly.

"I'm sure she will be," said Kate. She glanced down at a package in her hands. "Oh, I nearly forgot," she murmured. "This is for you."

Kara grimaced. "I can't take it. I can hardly even move."

"I didn't mean—" said Kate quickly. "It's just a little gift—a couple of books I thought you might enjoy reading. Shall I open it for you?"

"No. You can leave it on the nightstand," said Kara, allowing her disinterest to show. Why should she give an inch to Catherine Hardin?

With a vague, apologetic gesture, Aunt Kate put the present aside. Her eyes moistened unexpectedly.

Oh, no, not tears!—not from Aunt Kate! thought Kara in alarm.

Fortunately, the glistening eyes turned to a sparkle as Catherine smiled and said, "Kara, I care deeply about you and your mother. Please believe me. I want to do whatever I can to help."

Kara could tolerate no more of Kate's sappy pretense of concern. Her voice trembled as she challenged, "How can you say you care? You didn't even bother to attend my father's funeral!"

Catherine's expression clouded. "I—I couldn't—"

"Didn't you stop to think that your own sister would need you?"

"If I had thought so, I would have come," said Kate simply.

Kara looked away, her eyes tracing a crack on the far wall. Bitterly, in a rush of words, she said, "You've never shown the slightest concern for any of us, Aunt Kate. And now it's too late. Anna fell apart after Dad died. Her life ended with his. And so did mine."

"That's not so," said Catherine. "You have a long, wonderful life ahead of you."

"And Anna?"

Catherine sighed. "I pray to God she'll be all right. I really believe she will." Kate forced a smile and her voice brightened. "I want you to come home with me, Kara. I want to take care of you until you're on your feet again."

Kara scrutinized her aunt. "You mean, go live in your house in Claremont?"

"Yes, I'd love to have you."

"I can't."

"Well, not right away, of course. But as soon as the doctor releases you in a week or so."

"I don't want to go."

"But—what will you do?"

"I—I can go home—" Kara swallowed her words as she realized in dismay what she had said. "Home . . . our house," she repeated slowly. She looked at Kate. "Tell me, is there anything left?"

Catherine seemed reluctant to answer. "I don't know what's left," she said at last, "but I don't think you can go back."

"No," agreed Kara dryly, closing her eyes to block the prospect of tears. "We can never go back, can we?"

"It's usually better that we don't," observed Kate quietly.

What do you know about it? Kara wanted to demand. *You who sit in your perfect little ivory tower in Claremont, never soiling your hands with other people's problems!* But Kara said nothing. Her eyes remained closed even when Aunt Kate spoke again.

"I'll let your doctor know that you'll be coming home with me," she said, as if Kara had already agreed.

"I told you no!" Kara said sharply.

Kate's voice remained even, unruffled. "I'll let you think about it for a while, Kara. There's nothing I can do right now to help Anna . . . except to take care of you. I know it's what your mother would want." She turned to go, adding, "I'll be back tomorrow for your answer."

Kara had another visitor that afternoon: Dr. Lasky. He shuffled over to her bed and sat down heavily in his usual chair.

"Busy, busy day," he said with a grim smile, then added lightly, almost offhandedly, "How's my girl?"

"Okay. The pain isn't as bad."

He nodded approvingly. "You look a mite perkier than you did a couple of days ago."

"When can I go ho—" She caught herself. "I mean, leave the hospital?"

"You keep on improving like you are and I'll release you into your aunt's care in a few days."

"No," said Kara flatly. "I'm not staying with Aunt Kate."

Dr. Lasky made a pyramid with his fingertips, then reflectively touched the apex to his lips. He made a grunting sound low in his throat. His way of expressing his disapproval, surmised Kara.

"Aunt Kate has always avoided our family," she argued—pointlessly, she realized, since the doctor hadn't even replied yet. "I think there were hard feelings between my mother and her sister ever since they were young," Kara persisted. "The few times we saw her, I sensed an awful tension between Anna and Aunt Kate."

"Do you have somewhere else to go?" inquired Dr. Lasky in his formal physician's voice.

"No," admitted Kara.

"Then it's either stay here or be discharged into your aunt's care." He added, "I'm only doing what I know your father would want me to do."

Kara didn't reply. She knew there would be no swaying the good doctor. He was as stubborn about some things as her father had been. She looked at the gruff but kindly man and felt a brief surge of tenderness. He had been a part of her life for as long as her own parents. In fact, eighteen years ago he had delivered her!

"Now about Anna," he said, breaking into her thoughts.

"Oh, yes—Anna! Can I see her now?"

"Not yet. But soon. As soon as you're strong enough to navigate around this place on your own." He pursed his lips thoughtfully. "I do want to explain some things to you about her treatment."

"Dr. Lasky, whatever you're going to tell me, please be totally honest. I want the truth. Remember, I am a doctor's daughter."

"Yes, Kara, I will be frank. Your mother suffered what we call full-thickness burns."

"What does that mean?"

"All of her skin was destroyed on over thirty percent of her body, plus some of the underlying tissue and muscles."

Kara sucked in a deep breath and expelled it slowly. "That sounds terribly serious. Will . . . will she be all right?"

"Yes, it's very serious but not hopeless. It's true her wounds cannot heal by themselves, but we do have excellent grafting techniques to help the skin function normally again . . . in time."

"I see," said Kara. "When can you begin the grafting?"

"Not for several weeks yet. You see, Anna faces three phases of treatment. Actually, she's come through the first, which we call the emergent period. That included the first twenty-four hours after admittance. We determined the severity of her injuries and completed our initial fluid therapy. Your mother held her own through that period and is now in what we call the acute period."

"What does that mean?" asked Kara. "Is she getting better?"

"In a sense, yes. But you must keep in mind that this period may last for some time—until all of your mother's wounds are covered with grafts."

"How long do you think it will take?"

"Several months, at least. Probably longer," replied Dr. Lasky quietly. He added, "We have two goals for your mother during this time—to remove the eschar, or dead skin, as soon as possible, and begin grafting; and second, to avoid complications."

"Complications?"

Dr. Lasky put a gentle hand on Kara's. "My dear, all severe burns result in complications. I'm afraid complications are the rule rather than the exception."

"What sort of complications?"

"I don't think you need to be concerned with them—at the moment. Anna may not experience any of them."

"But you just said it's likely she will. I want to know. What are they?"

"Very well. Pneumonia . . . septicemia . . . kidney failure . . . heart disease. They're the most common problems."

Kara was thoughtful. "I think I remember hearing, from my father or somewhere, that infection is the leading cause of death in burn patients."

"That's right. Anna faces a double challenge. Not only has her body lost its protection against infection, but it must also attempt to repair wounds larger than it is capable of handling.'' He paused, cleared his throat, and patted her hand reassuringly. ''But we'll give our Anna every help available.''

''Will it be enough?''

''Anna is strong. If she helps us half as much as we help her—''

A frown creased Kara's brow. ''Anna was in an awful mood before the fire. She hasn't recovered from Dad's death.''

''I suspected that. We'll just have to do all we can to encourage her.''

''Dr. Lasky, you mentioned three phases. What is the last one?''

''That's the rehabilitation period, in which we work at returning Anna to a normal, useful, fulfilling life. Let me reassure you, Kara, most people do recover from severe burns, both functionally and emotionally.''

Kara gave him an inquisitive glance. ''Do you really believe Anna will recover . . . emotionally?''

Dr. Lasky gave her a warm, paternal smile. ''We'll see, dear. Your mother may surprise us all.''

''I want to see her, Dr. Lasky,'' said Kara suddenly. ''Please.''

''Very well. Day after tomorrow—if you both are up to it.''

———

Dr. Lasky kept his promise. Two days later he appeared in Kara's room with a nurse, and they helped her out of bed. ''We'll walk partway,'' he told her, ''but Miss Griffin will follow with a wheelchair if you find yourself tiring.''

''I won't,'' promised Kara as the nurse gently helped her into her robe. ''They've had me up several times the last two days. I feel myself getting stronger.''

''All well and good,'' he said, supporting her with his arm as she shuffled into the hallway. The distance to the burn ward looked immense, but at least Miss Griffin was following at a reassuring distance with the chair. Halfway there, Kara felt her legs weaken distressingly. As her step wavered, Dr. Lasky gripped her and helped her into the wheelchair. She rode the rest of the way in resigned silence.

At the door to the burn unit, as Dr. Lasky picked up clean scrub gowns for Kara and himself, he said, "Don't expect too much of her yet, Kara. Patients with serious burns are often only semi-responsive for the first few weeks. A bit of confusion and disorientation is normal."

"Are you trying to prepare me for something, Dr. Lasky?" asked Kara. She stood up uncertainly as the nurse slipped the sterile gown over her bathrobe.

"There you are, Miss Strickland," said the nurse, tying it at the back.

Kara murmured, "Thank you," but kept her eyes on the doctor. With only a nod, he opened the door and they went in. The large room smelled of an unsettling mixture of disinfectants and the pungent, unmistakable odor of damaged flesh. Kara caught her breath when she spied Anna in one of the open cubicles, lying propped up in bed, her body seemingly pinned down by a web of tubes, catheters, and monitoring devices.

It was Anna, and yet it could have been someone else— a dark, shrunken, distorted image of her mother. Her chest and arms were wrapped in thick gauze dressings. A white sheet covered her from the waist down. The gaunt face turned slightly and Anna's dark pinpoint eyes glimmered momentarily with recognition. Dr. Lasky helped Kara over to the bedside.

"Anna . . . Mother? It's me, Kara."

"Kara? Are you . . . all right?" said Anna, forming the words with effort.

"Yes, I'm fine, just fine," said Kara, blinking to keep back tears.

"I waited for you for so long," Anna moaned. "You should have come sooner." Her voice grew stronger as she said, "Now you must tell them, Kara. Tell them!"

Kara looked questioningly at Dr. Lasky. "Tell who . . . what?"

"Tell them to let me go home. I want to go home, Kara. Tell them they can't keep me here."

Dr. Lasky stepped forward and said soothingly, "Now, Anna, we've talked about this before. When you're all well, then you can go home—"

Anna's eyes grew glazed, unfocused. "I'll tell Ben on you," she murmured. "You wait. I'll tell Ben. He'll let me go home."

Kara searched Dr. Lasky's eyes as he slowly guided her away from Anna's bed. "She won't always be like this, will she?"

"No, not at all. In fact, months from now she probably won't even remember these first few weeks."

"But what makes her so confused?"

"We call it burn encephalopathy. There can be any combination of contributing factors—smoke inhalation, shock, medication, even Anna's own emotional stability before the fire."

"Or lack of it?"

"Yes, especially that."

"Kara, come back," called Anna, her voice rising in desperation. "Get me my clothes . . . my red dress. Please help me!"

"Should I stay with her . . . try to reason with her?" Kara asked anxiously.

The doctor piloted her toward the door. "No, Kara. I think we should let her rest now."

"Kara, you come here!" came Anna's voice, alarming and shrill. "You take me home, Kara. Take me home now!"

Once outside the burn unit, Kara sank gratefully into the

wheelchair and allowed herself to be wheeled back to her room. On the way, she gazed up sadly at Dr. Lasky. "I only upset her, didn't I?"

The doctor ground his jaw slightly. He didn't reply.

"Why should seeing me make her so upset?" persisted Kara.

Dr. Lasky appeared profoundly absorbed in thought. Then he caught himself and murmured vaguely, "We'll give her some time, Kara. A little time."

———

Three days later Catherine Hardin came to take Kara to her home in Claremont. Kara was beyond protesting. She had allowed her mind to go numb, to slip into a state of wordless acquiescence. She would allow herself to be shepherded about, cared for and attended to, without complaint or rebuke. Why argue? It would accomplish nothing. For the time being, her life had been taken out of her own hands. Until she was fully recovered she would have to go along for the ride— even if that meant enduring the coddling hospitality of Aunt Kate.

Kara and Catherine saw Anna only briefly before they left the hospital. Anna was sleeping fitfully. They were careful not to awaken her.

Dr. Lasky himself wheeled Kara out to the hospital parking lot, although she kept insisting she could walk. "Hospital policy," he said firmly. He helped Kara into the waiting automobile, then turned to Catherine. "You have the list of instructions for outpatient care, don't you, Kate?" he asked. It seemed odd to Kara, hearing Dr. Lasky use Kate's family name instead of Catherine or Miss Hardin.

"I have the list right here," said Kate, patting her purse. "Miss Griffin gave me a supply of gauze bandages, and I have your prescription for the appropriate salves and creams."

"Good, good. You'll be a nurse yet." He looked back at

Kara with an expression of inexplicable gentleness. "Kara, my girl, you'll be fine. Change those dressings daily. Stay out of the sun. Wear loose clothing for a few weeks. And eat lots of proteins and carbohydrates."

Kara nodded.

"I'll see you back here for a checkup in two weeks."

"She'll be here," said Kate, starting the engine. She craned her neck toward Dr. Lasky. "Take care of Anna. Call us if there's . . . anything at all."

With a final wave, Kate pulled out into the street. The next two hours were excruciating for Kara. Although Kate drove well, the slightest bumps and turns irritated Kara's wounds. She said nothing, though, keeping her lips tightly clamped, refusing to share even her pain with Aunt Kate.

Shortly before dusk, Catherine pulled into the driveway of a large white frame house—a faded, rambling two-story with a pointed roof and a wide, covered porch with blocklike pillars. Kara hadn't seen the house in years. The double windows were shutterless, framed by narrow strips of wood. Venetian blinds gave the structure a private, austere quality, not ominous, but not especially inviting either.

Catherine got out of the car and looked back at Kara. "I'll go unlock the door and come back for you," she explained. Kara nodded, deliberately avoiding her aunt's eyes.

While Kate worked with the door, Kara gazed curiously through the sun-streaked windshield at the house. It seemed almost nondescript in its staid, settled, barren surroundings. Two trees stood like sentries, one at each side of the house. Kara wondered at them. It was the middle of summer. Why so few leaves, so little greenery? The expansive yard, too, was a patchwork of brown and anemic green—sparse, scattered clumps of grass struggling through stubborn soil. It occurred to Kara that it was probably difficult for a woman living alone, and no doubt working full time, to care properly for such a large yard. But surely the fastidious Kate could hire someone.

In a sense, the whole place was a relic, Kara reflected somberly. She thought of the phrase "a relic from the past." This was it, all right. Maybe that was what Aunt Kate was too.

Kara recalled that Anna and Kate had grown up together in this house. Perhaps they had climbed those trees and played school on the front porch steps. The idea of Anna and Kate playing together as children struck Kara as improbable, even absurd. As adults they were strangers to each other. Could they ever have been close? Their personalities, too, were so opposite in nature. Catherine, a devout woman, prim and proper, gave the impression of a puritanical lifestyle, perfectly controlled; while Anna—oh, poor, dear Anna—had she ever been at peace? Had she ever possessed even a measure of genuine self-confidence? To Kara she had always seemed fretful, high-strung, and—since losing her husband—nearly mad, bent on self-destruction. Yes, recalled Kara soberly, Anna had nearly accomplished that—for both of them.

"Kara. Kara? Are you ready?" Aunt Kate was leaning into the car, offering her arms for support.

"What? Oh, yes, I'm sorry," said Kara. "I was . . . just thinking."

"You certainly were," Catherine agreed as she carefully eased Kara out of the vehicle. "Do you remember the house? You were only a child the last time you were here."

"I remember a little," said Kara vaguely. She had no wish to remember, nor to think of anything at all. She wished suddenly that she could wipe her mind clean like a slate, forgetting how drastically her life had changed. She didn't want to anticipate living with Aunt Kate in her ugly old house in a strange town, away from her friends and from Anna. Most of all, Kara didn't want to think about who she was now and what she would do with the rest of her life . . . whatever was left of it.

5

Aunt Kate's house was infinitely more impressive on the inside than the outside. The living room was tastefully decorated with richly grained oak tables, elegant wing chairs, and a graceful, floral-print Chippendale love seat and sofa, similar to ones Anna had owned. From where she stood, Kara could see in the dining room a lovely large buffet and an exquisite tea wagon. And in the adjoining study bookshelves spanned an entire wall, with surely enough reading material to last a lifetime.

Kara moved across the room with slow, precise steps, taking in everything, noticing how the rooms were attractively accented by tapered candles and fine china cups, by oil paintings and ornate mirrors, and by bowls of ripe fruit and freshly cut flowers. She wanted to exclaim that she adored the house, but pride and an unspoken resentment silenced her. So, instead, she feigned disinterest and loathed herself for it. There was so much she wanted to see and inquire about. But she refused to admit aloud that her own tastes and preferences matched Aunt Catherine's.

"I hope you'll feel at home here, Kara," said Kate, tentatively offering her hand for support.

"I'm very tired," said Kara, ignoring the hand. "Where will I be staying?"

"Your room is here, downstairs," said Catherine, "so you won't have far to walk."

"I don't remember much about the house—inside, I mean."

"You were very young last time you were here. Basically the place hasn't changed since your grandparents lived here. Of course, over the years I've added touches of my own."

"It's very nice," conceded Kara.

They made their way down the hall to the second door—a pretty, cheerful room done in pale greens. A large old-fashioned doll with red hair and a frilly dress sat on the fluffy white bedspread.

Catherine went over, picked up the doll, and held it as if it were a private treasure. "This belonged to Anna or me, I can't remember which," she volunteered with just a hint of self-consciousness. "We had identical dolls, but one broke, so we shared the one that remained." Tenderly she replaced the doll and gazed at Kara. "Did you know your mother and I were very close as children?"

Kara considered challenging such a preposterous remark, but she felt too weary to expend the effort. Besides, perhaps Aunt Kate was telling the truth. But then, if so, what—or who—had driven such an immovable wedge between the two women?

———

The next few days passed without incident, taking on, in fact, a pleasant, rosy sort of sameness. Catherine was attentive, even overly solicitous of Kara's needs. She plied Kara with sumptuous meals, faithfully changed her dressings, fluffed her pillows, and brought her magazines and books.

Kara couldn't help but be impressed. Her own mother couldn't have shown more loving concern. Of course, Anna had never quite fit the motherly mold of cuddling and coddling, which was perhaps one reason Kara had turned so unreservedly to her father for affection.

Kara had time to think of him now—her father, Ben

Strickland. Too much time. The memories came swiftly, sharply, bringing pain, and left as quickly, leaving emptiness. She missed him now more than ever.

Involuntarily, to compensate for her loneliness, Kara turned increasingly to Aunt Catherine. As the days passed, the two women slipped into a routine of sitting together on the front porch after dinner to escape the closed-in heat of the house. Kara found herself gradually letting down her defenses, cautiously sharing some of her feelings and experiences with Aunt Kate. Kate was a ready, eager listener.

One day as Catherine applied salve to Kara's arms, Kara said, "You've cared for me for well over a week now, Aunt Kate, but don't you have a job somewhere? Don't you have to go to work?"

Catherine smiled, "Of course I work. But I took my vacation. When you've worked in a place for fifteen years, they figure you can handle three weeks of vacation a year."

"You mean you took your vacation just to care for me?" protested Kara.

"I don't mind," laughed Kate, "so why should you?"

"But your vacation—"

"I had nothing else planned . . . and nowhere to go."

"It sounds like you lead a rather solitary existence," ventured Kara.

"I do," said Kate, "but I stay busy with my job and church activities, so I manage quite well actually."

"What is your job?" queried Kara. She paused and, in embarrassment, added, "I just realized I haven't the slightest idea what you do."

"I'm a designer with the Kramer Corporation here in town. I design greeting cards."

"Oh, then you're an artist."

"Of sorts. I do some drawing, but mainly lay-out work. It's fun."

"I bet you did all the paintings in this house."

"Some of them. But most were done by your grandfather. He was quite an artist himself."

"I never knew him," mused Kara.

"No. He died shortly after . . . after you were born," said Catherine pensively. "Mother followed a year later . . . of a broken heart, I suspect."

"That's just how Anna has taken my dad's death," said Kara. "She's been inconsolable."

"She loved Ben very much."

"So did I," reflected Kara, the familiar grief creeping into her voice. "More than any other person on earth."

"I think pain is the other side of love," said Catherine softly.

"But lately it hurts even more," said Kara.

"Perhaps because you've been confined too long. You need to get out and do things and see people."

Kara looked doubtfully at her bandaged arms. "No, Aunt Kate, I can't see anyone yet."

"Yes, you can," said Kate with determined enthusiasm. "You can wear long sleeves. I have several blouses you can have. We're about the same size. And I have a lovely lace shawl. You can wear it to church with me this Sunday."

"No, really, I can't—"

"Please, Kara. It's just a little church, nothing fancy or elaborate. And nice, friendly people. I really would like you to join me."

"I don't know when I was last in a church," said Kara, flustered. "Perhaps for . . . for Dad's funeral. You see, I have no beliefs . . . what you call faith."

Catherine smiled and said, "We all live by faith, Kara—in ourselves, in fate, in our world system, or in God. The question is not whether you have faith, but where you place it."

"Then I suppose my faith is in myself," replied Kara simply.

"Just the same, I'd be pleased if you'd accompany me to church on Sunday."

Against her better judgment, Kara agreed to go. But on Sunday morning her reservations weighed heavily on her. Was she ready yet to cope with people—their questions, their stares, their likely uneasiness around her? Her singed hair was still uneven, unmanageable, and too short. Her face wasn't burned, but it still looked as if she had been out in the sun too long. And her hands—they were no longer smooth and white, but rough and red. Would they ever be attractive again? Would she?

With growing misgivings, Kara slipped into the front seat of the car beside Aunt Kate. Minutes later they arrived at the little white stucco church—an amazing replica of the traditional country church in Christmas greeting cards. Kate and Kara entered the sanctuary just as the congregation stood to sing. They chose a back pew, as close to the exit as Kara could manage. She figured if the service became unendurable, she could steal out quietly.

But to her own surprise, Kara found herself enjoying the organ music and the hymns. The people sang energetically, with obvious feeling. Several of the songs seemed distantly familiar, although Kara couldn't imagine where she had heard them. Still, they sparked warm feelings inside her.

The sermon was another matter. Kara was appalled. The minister expounded vigorously for over half an hour on the blood of Jesus. The blood of Jesus! Incredible! Why not His wisdom, His moral teachings, His example?

Kara grew warm and restless. A dozen times she imagined herself getting up and going out the exit. But each time she also envisioned dozens of curious eyes turning her way. Where is she going? Is the poor thing sick? Oh, look—the bandages! So she kept her seat and tried grudgingly to focus on the minister's words.

"Jesus was wounded for our transgressions. . . . He was

bruised for our iniquities," boomed the thick-browed, barrel-chested man from his pulpit.

Kara pictured Christ, His flesh pierced and bleeding, then thought with momentary revulsion of her own oozing, ulcerous wounds. And Anna's! Why had *they* been scarred? What purpose had God served by wounding them? No, Kara could not conceive of such a callous, capricious God, allowing people to suffer—even His own Son.

She told Aunt Kate so as they drove home from church. Kate calmly refuted her. "Sin brought death and suffering into the world, Kara, not God."

"It doesn't make sense," argued Kara. "If there is a God, then He could simply say a word and erase all the world's pain and suffering."

"No," said Kate," because then He wouldn't be a God of justice."

"Justice? That's a . . . a rather old-fashioned word, isn't it?"

"It just means that someone must pay for the sins that we commit. It's a basic law of life. We see it every day."

Kara couldn't argue with that. Anna's weakness had caused the fire. Both Kara and Anna would pay for that act of folly—or insanity—for the rest of their lives. She recalled that the minister had used the phrase, "The wages of sin is death. . . ." Kara said the words aloud, solemnly, and felt a chill in her bones. "It sounds so final, " she murmured.

Kate glanced over at her, then back at the road. "There's more to the verse, Kara. Do you remember it?"

"No, I don't."

"The rest of the verse says, '. . . but the gift of God is eternal life through Jesus Christ our Lord.' You see, Kara, God does love us. He wants us to be happy."

"Happy?" echoed Kara skeptically. "I don't know what happiness is anymore."

The shadow of a smile played on Catherine's lips. "One

thing I learned a long time ago, Kara, is that sometimes we create our own unhappiness. And I'll share something else with you. Over the years I've found my only real happiness in God."

Kara remained silent, mulling over a peculiar ambivalence taking shape in her mind—an impatient wish to dismiss her aunt's words as the foolish prattling of a fanatical old maid, and, incredibly, a seed of yearning to believe in Catherine's God.

6

*O*n Tuesday Aunt Kate drove Kara back to Westchester for her two-week checkup. As they approached the city, Kara said, "Would you please drive by the house? I want to see it."

Catherine looked doubtful. "Do you think you should? I'm afraid there isn't much left."

"I have to see what's there. The fire is like a dream—a nightmare—in my mind. At night it keeps coming back to haunt me. But in the daylight it's not real. I have to face it. I have to see the house as it is now."

"But we don't want to be late for your appointment—"

"It's not till two. Please, Aunt Kate, it's only a little out of your way. And I don't want to face this alone. I want you with me."

Kate nodded reluctantly. "I just don't want to see you upset."

They circled around and drove down the familiar tree-lined streets to the Strickland address. Everything in the neighborhood looked the same, reassuringly normal—houses busy with activity, children playing, teenage boys washing their cars, the sun streaming over flower beds and green, well-manicured lawns.

Then, as the car pulled to a stop, Kara saw it—a gaping black hole in the lovely pastel canvas. She stared incredulously at the stark, charred skeleton of rubble and debris that was once her home. "Oh, no, please, it can't be!" she moaned, turning imploringly to Catherine.

Tears dampened Kate's face too as she gently rubbed the back of Kara's neck. "You're a strong person. You and your mother will begin again . . . you'll go on from here."

"But there's nothing left. Everything's gone."

"You have each other," said Kate soothingly. "That's more than some people ever have."

Kara sat back, dried her eyes, and struggled to regain her composure. "I'm ready to go on to the hospital, Aunt Kate. I want to see Anna now."

They drove the short distance in silence. Then, while Kara kept her appointment with Dr. Lasky, Catherine visited Anna. A half hour later, Kara and Kate met outside the burn unit.

"How was your checkup?" asked Kate.

"Fine." Kara extended her arms. "See? No more bandages. Dr. Lasky says in time the scars will hardly show."

"That's wonderful news."

"How was Anna?" asked Kara, her voice sounding less confident.

"All right, I suppose. But she's still not herself. She seems a bit incoherent . . . out of touch with reality."

"Dr. Lasky warned me about that," said Kara. "He said Anna swings between periods of lucidity and confusion. She's been very depressed about her condition."

"That's certainly understandable," said Kate.

"Dr. Lasky said she may be suffering from what he calls acute brain syndrome. He says many burn patients experience it to some degree."

"Is it serious?"

"I don't think so. At least it's not permanent. As Anna's body heals, her mind will clear. Dr. Lasky said several things could cause her confusion—her medications, an electrolyte imbalance, dehydration, fear, the trauma of the burn itself."

Catherine patted Kara's arm. "Well, as long as we know her condition's only temporary."

"I'd better go in to see her now," said Kara. "Do you want to come back in too?"

"No," replied Kate. "I think one visitor at a time is enough. I'll go down to the cafeteria for some coffee."

"Okay. I'll meet you there."

Kara slipped into a sterile gown, then entered the burn ward, steeling herself for the inevitable sense of repugnance she would feel. The familiar grim sights and foul smells assaulted her again, but she was stronger this time, better able to cope with them. She realized that she needed to be strong for Anna, so that somehow, in time, the two of them could pull their lives back together.

She approached Anna's bedside with a determined smile. "Hello, Anna," she said softly. "I missed you. You're looking stronger."

Her mother turned her head slightly toward her, but her eyes remained closed. "Catherine?" she murmured.

"No, it's me, Kara."

"Kara?" Anna reached out her hand as far as the bandages would permit.

"Yes, I'm right here, Mother," said Kara, taking the frail hand.

"Catherine," said Anna urgently, her eyes opening to reveal glazed pupils, "you must leave Kara alone, do you hear?"

"Anna, I'm Kara. Don't you understand?" She forced a brightness into her voice. "Aunt Kate and I are getting along fine, Mother. She's much nicer than I had imagined."

Anna gripped Kara's hand with surprising strength and said more urgently, "If I take Kara, you must promise to leave her alone. You are never to see her, and you are never to tell her who you are. Do you promise?"

"Anna, you're not making any sense," cried Kara, attempting to pull away.

Anna held her firm. The words rushed from her lips in a crazed, demanding hiss. "Do you understand, Catherine?

Kara will be mine—my child—and you must never try to take her back!"

Kara drew back, stunned. She stared at Anna. "W— What are you saying?"

Anna lapsed into a state of garbled whimpering. She turned her head away and groaned, "Someone please help me. It hurts. Don't leave me here."

"Anna, what did you mean?" demanded Kara. "What about Aunt Kate taking me back? Do you mean now—my staying with her?" Kara's voice rose precariously. "Why did you say I'd be your child? Of course, I'm your—" She paused, and a sudden blast of comprehension thrust inward upon her senses. She covered her mouth in horror. "Oh, dear God, no!"

She leaned down and peered intently at Anna, turning Anna's face until their eyes met. "Is that it—what you're saying?—I'm not your child?"

Anna's eyes closed. "Someone help me," she mumbled.

Kara turned away, her mind numb, dazed. She left the burn unit and discarded her scrub gown. Her thoughts churned with the implications of Anna's words.

Who am I? Who is my mother?

She walked blindly down the hall, moving as though in a dream. She bumped into an empty gurney, then nearly collided with a hospital worker pushing a cart of dinner trays.

"Excuse me," Kara said vaguely, awkwardly sidestepping the woman.

"Are you all right, miss?"

Kara didn't reply. Spotting Dr. Lasky emerging from a patient's room, she called his name with a tone of stunned desperation.

Immediately the doctor turned and looked at her. When she reached him, he opened his arms and enfolded her. "My dear child, what has happened? Is it Anna?"

"No—yes," she sobbed. "I mean, I don't know."

"Come, let's talk," he said, guiding her over to a nearby visitors' lounge. "See, there's no one here now. We can talk freely."

Kara sank into a chair and fished in her purse for a tissue. "I—I saw Anna," she began haltingly. "She told me . . . she said—"

Dr. Lasky put a comforting hand on Kara's arm. "Take it easy, dear. You know, I told you Anna might not be quite rational."

Kara blew her nose, then sat for a minute in silence until her breathing became more regular. When she spoke again, her voice was stronger, calmer. "Dr. Lasky, you've been our family doctor since before I was born—"

"That's right, I have," he said agreeably. "In fact, I delivered you myself."

"Then you know . . . you can tell me—"

"Tell you what, dear?" he asked, smiling encouragingly.

She swallowed hard, then said the words with a deadly precision. "Whose daughter am I? Anna's—or Catherine's?"

Dr. Lasky's smile died on his lips. He coughed harshly, as if to clear the atmosphere of the poison she had just exuded. "What makes you think—?" he began, but Kara's expression told him she wouldn't tolerate evasiveness. He sighed deeply, as if she had placed upon him a weight too heavy to bear. "That's a question you'll have to ask your mother," he said at last, gravely.

Kara's voice escaped, too shrill, too frantic. "But, Dr. Lasky, who *is* my mother?"

7

Aunt Kate was speaking, her voice light and quick, her tone sweetly cajoling. But her words were winging like darts over Kara's head—meaningless, irritating. A wall of numbness blocked Kara's comprehension. She sat motionless, her eyes riveted to the highway as Catherine's car propelled them back to Claremont.

I have to ask her, thought Kara darkly. *I have to know the truth.*

"Shall we stop somewhere for dinner?" suggested Kate cheerily. "I think both of us could use a good meal."

"No, I'm not hungry," said Kara, her voice brusque, querulous.

Kate glanced quizzically at her. "Are you feeling okay?"

"Yes, all right, considering . . ."

Kate nodded sympathetically. "I guess today has been pretty rough on you—first seeing the house and then Anna. If it's any consolation, I really believe Anna will make it. My sister has a will of iron."

Kara made no reply. She stared out the window, willing herself away, anywhere but in the close confines of this vehicle with Aunt Kate. Or should she say Mother? Kara nervously massaged her marred, reddened hands. She had to speak, had to confront Catherine. But how? When?

"How about picking up something at a fast-food place—maybe a hamburger and a shake?" urged Kate. "We really do need to eat."

"You can stop if you want," said Kara dully. She knew that stopping would only prolong the agony of not knowing, the torment of questions in her mind. One question—and depending on its answer, perhaps a million more.

Are you my mother? Then how . . . when . . . why!

"There's a place to eat," said Kate, breaking into Kara's reverie. She swerved into a driveway and pulled to a stop beside a small drive-in restaurant. "I know it looks like a greasy spoon," she said, tossing Kara an apologetic grin, "but it's better than starving. They do have indoor seating. Shall we go in?"

"I suppose it beats juggling food in the car," said Kara, opening her door.

"I always spill something when I try to eat in the car," laughed Kate. "The spots on the upholstery aren't part of the original decor, you know!"

Kara managed a faint, dutiful laugh, which only caused Kate to eye her questioningly as they entered the restaurant. They placed their order at the counter, collected their food, then sat down in a small booth with uncomfortable wooden seats. No cushions. No air conditioning. Just loud, jarring music blaring from speakers on the wall—a popular rock number, heavy on the drums and screeching electronic effects. Kara, nibbling her paper-thin hamburger, noted that the lead singer was screaming above the raucous clamor of the instruments. The winner was a draw, she decided, but the loser was clearly the listener!

"More french fries?" said Kate, pushing the cardboard carton toward Kara.

"No thanks."

Kate looked at her with undisguised concern. "Try not to worry about your mother," she said gently.

"I'm not," said Kara. She sipped her shake before inadvertently saying more.

They arrived home around nine P.M. Not really *home*,

Kara reminded herself severely. It was Catherine Hardin's home—whoever Catherine Hardin was. For the moment she was a mystery—what did they call it?—a conundrum, a puzzle. It was up to Kara now to unravel it. But would she at the same time be unraveling what was left of her own life, crushing—and cursing—her personal victory with a single question? Perhaps. But it was a chance she had to take.

"Would you like some iced tea?" Kate asked her as they entered the kitchen.

"No, but I—I would like to talk to you," ventured Kara.

Kate's expression brightened. "Of course. I'd love for us to sit down and have a talk."

"I don't need to sit down."

"Oh, surely, let's be comfortable. I'll get my tea and we'll relax on the sofa in the living room."

"I have just one question," said Kara curtly. "I can ask it right here."

Catherine fixed her with a curious gaze. "Of course, dear. What is it?"

Kara felt herself retreating slightly. Suppose Anna's remarks were nothing more than the insane rantings of a delirious woman?

"What did you want to ask me?" repeated Kate, sipping her tea.

Kara grasped the back of a kitchen chair for support. "Anna said some things . . . she was only rambling perhaps."

"Rambling—?"

"Yes—I don't know. She said . . . it was incredible—"

"Tell me, Kara."

Kara caught her breath and blurted recklessly, "Aunt Kate, are you my mother?"

Catherine remained motionless, frozen in a gesture of relaxed conviviality, her tea glass raised halfway to her lips. For an instant Kara thought her aunt would crumble where she stood, but finally Kate appeared to shake off her astonishment. Trembling slightly, she set her glass on the table, looked directly at Kara, and said quietly, "Yes . . . I am your mother."

Kara had not really expected this reply. Surely it had played in her mind as a possibility, perhaps even probable, but until this moment the idea had lacked substance, authenticity. Now, verified, it slammed against her brain with the stunning, dizzying impact of truth. Kara's knees weakened. Desperately her fingers gripped the chair. She bit her lip, wishing she could retrieve her stupid, devastating question. But it was too late. Already a myriad of ensuing questions were bombarding her mind. Still, she could only manage to utter dumbly, "I didn't know . . ."

"I know," said Kate. "We couldn't tell you. It's a very long, complicated story."

"I—I want to hear it," Kara said faintly.

Kate picked up her glass of tea. "I'll tell you everything, but let's go sit down first."

They went to the living room and sat down, Kate on the sofa, Kara in a straight-back chair. Kate was silent for a minute, pulling a wisp of auburn hair behind her ear, apparently sifting memories and gathering her thoughts. Then, turning her glass slowly in her hands, she said, "When your mother and I were young, I dated your father, Ben Strickland, for several months. I liked him well enough, and I believe he cared a great deal for me. But I was more interested in someone else, a young man who attended the university. He was a fascinating person who dreamed of someday becoming a famous author and who talked of taking me with him to exotic places. I fell deeply in love with him and his dreams."

Catherine paused, her eyes growing wistful with unspoken, bittersweet memories. Then she caught herself and looked somberly at Kara. "By the time I found out I was pregnant," she said, her tone grave, "he was already weaving dreams with another girl—someone in one of his classes at college."

"But didn't he know?" queried Kara.

"I never told him about the baby," replied Kate. "I was ashamed and frantic, and petrified at the thought of bringing disgrace to my family."

"What did you do?"

"Nothing, at first. By then your father had begun to date my sister. After a whirlwind courtship, Ben and Anna were married. They had a beautiful, impressive wedding. It was such a happy time for our family, I didn't want to spoil it." Kate sighed heavily. "But finally I had to tell them. . . ."

Kara sat forward slightly. "What happened then?"

"Oh, they were very supportive and understanding. In fact, Ben and Anna took me in and cared for me until the baby—you were born. We talked about it over and over, and we all agreed that it would be best for you if Ben and Anna adopted you as their own daughter."

Kara broke in. "So you just handed me over and . . . and stepped out of my life for good, just like that?"

"No," said Kate. "After you were born, I cared for you until you were nearly two. Anna and Ben were kind enough to let me stay on with them. They knew how much I wanted to be with you, even though I couldn't acknowledge you as my child."

"But I thought you and Anna didn't get along well. You've always avoided each other."

"I know, but it wasn't that way until . . . until you began to call me Mommy. You were just a baby, not even two, and we had confused you. You must have thought you had two mothers. Then, when you began turning more often to me, Anna decided I should leave and have as little as possible to do with your life."

Solemnly Kara said, "So you walked out and never came back."

Kate's voice broke with emotion. "We never wanted you to know, Kara. We wanted you to grow up with a normal life, like other children. I never wanted you to suffer because of my mistake."

Kara ran her hand distractedly through her long, auburn-brown hair. Her eyes narrowed ominously as she challenged, "Weren't you the thoughtful, self-sacrificing mother!" She stood up and walked over to the window, then turned sharply to face Kate. "How could you all play with my life like that—make decisions about me as if I were a—a possession you could just pass around?"

"It wasn't like that, Kara," said Kate. "I was so young, not much older than you are now." She shrugged helplessly. "We all wanted the best for you. We loved you very much."

"You make yourself sound so noble," snapped Kara. "Well, you make me sick. I feel physically ill, thinking of you as my mother. I hate it! I wish I didn't know." She bit her lower lip to keep it from quivering, then said shakily, "The fire destroyed my present and my future, and now you've destroyed my past. There's nothing left for me, nothing at all!"

Kate approached Kara, her arms outstretched to offer a comforting embrace. Kara turned away abruptly. Brushing away unwelcome tears, she stalked across the room to the hallway.

"Where are you going?" cried Catherine, surrendering to her own tears.

"I'm leaving this house," said Kara coldly. "I can't stay here with you. You pretend to be a Christian, so holy and good. You even had me feeling guilty because I couldn't be as pure and perfect as you. But you're a liar, Aunt Kate, and worse! You couldn't bear to live with your mistake, so you gave me away, your own child. How convenient for you! You go around acting like a saint. Oh, no one would ever guess you have an illegitimate daughter. But you have made my entire life a lie! And I'll hate you forever for that!"

Trembling, Kara ran to her room and slammed the door. She knew she had to get away. For her own sanity she had to escape from Catherine Hardin's house, although she had no idea where she would go without money at ten o'clock at night. With a sort of hypnotic desperation she went to the bedside telephone and called a cab. Surely she had enough cash for that. Then she quickly threw her few possessions into an overnight bag—mostly clothing and cosmetics Aunt Kate had given her. The fire had taken everything of Kara's. It was the ultimate shame—to have nothing she could call her own, not material goods, not her heritage, not even her name.

8

"Where to, lady?" The pudgy-faced taxi driver leaned one beefy elbow on the cushioned backrest and gazed at Kara with an expression of cool indifference. "You hear me, miss? I said, where to?"

"I—I don't know," said Kara haltingly from the backseat. "Perhaps a hotel . . . something not too expensive."

"What hotel, lady?"

She shrugged apologetically. "I don't know the name. I'm new in town. Would you know of one that's reasonably priced?"

The burly man's voice became gruff, condescending. "Lady, I ain't no tour guide. You tell me the address, I'll take you there."

Kara felt hot tears well up in her eyes. For a moment she felt an overwhelming desire to run back into the comforting security of Aunt Kate's house. But no. Never. "Is there a—a bus station in town?" she asked.

"A bus station? Sure. Only it ain't the best area, you know, for a girl alone at night."

"I don't know where else to go," she confessed.

The edge in the man's voice softened slightly. "Okay, miss, but remember, I warned ya." He shifted gears, jerked the battered, loose-jointed vehicle away from the curb, and roared down the street.

Twenty minutes later, when Kara entered the bus depot, she knew immediately that she should have listened to the taxi

driver. The shabby, nearly deserted building smelled of dirty
bathrooms and stale cigar smoke. The floors were dingy and
cluttered with trash. Two men sat reading newspapers, and a
frail, balding man sat behind the ticket counter writing something.

Kara sat down as unobtrusively as possible and picked
up a newspaper. Eagerly her eyes scanned the ads for rooms
or apartments to rent. She circled several possibilities, then
walked over to a large city map on the wall beside the ticket
counter. Painstakingly she located each address. Her heart
leaped with hope as she spotted an inexpensive bachelor
apartment only ten blocks from the bus station.

The ticket man craned his neck toward her and snorted,
"No more buses going out till four A.M."

"That's all right," said Kara meekly. "I'm not sure
where I'm going anyway." She didn't dare add that she had
come here because it was the only place open where she could
spend the night without paying.

She felt the eagle-eyed man's curious gaze on her as she
slipped noiselessly back to her seat. She lifted the newspaper
like a shield and hungrily searched the want ads. A job, that's
what she needed. If she had her own income, she would be
financially independent. She wouldn't have to depend on her
mother or Aunt Kate. (Oh, those old familiar designations:
mother . . . aunt. They were so firmly entrenched in her mind!
How could she ever uproot or reverse them? Better not to
think of them at all!)

Sometime around two A.M. Kara dozed off, her head loll-
ing back unsteadily on the straight, narrow bench. She awoke
abruptly at four when the bus rumbled in. Her neck was stiff,
her back ached, and her mouth tasted like flypaper. She went
to the rest room and splashed cold water on her face, but she
reluctantly decided she preferred her own discomfort to using
the squalid, dirt-encrusted facilities.

At six she got a candy bar and a can of cola from the

vending machine. *A delightful repast,* she mused ruefully, *and in such elegant surroundings!* As she ate, she noticed a toothless old man on the opposite bench grinning at her. Every time she swallowed, so did he. She could see his Adam's apple bob up and down with every bite. Kara grew increasingly self-conscious. Silently, furiously, she resolved, *No matter how wretched you make me feel, I'll pretend I don't see you, you leering old dotard!*

Finally, in desperation, Kara gathered her things, including her newspaper, and went outside where she could finish her drink in a semblance of privacy. It was morning at last. She breathed eagerly, cleansing her lungs with the chilly, damp air. This had been the longest night of her life—or nearly so, she reflected bitterly, recalling the tragic nights of the fire and of her father's death.

Unexpectedly she spied the old man stumbling out the depot door toward her. His watery gaze remained focused on her face.

I've got to get out of here! she thought wildly, starting to walk in the direction of the apartment building ten blocks away. With every block she increased her pace, feeling somehow the revolting presence of the old man dogging her. She had glanced back the first couple of blocks and had seen him—surely it was he—a musty, decrepit figure, somehow ominous, trudging some distance behind.

When Kara reached the apartment building on the corner of Olive and Bloomfield, she dodged inside, feeling weak and breathless but immensely relieved. (No matter that the building was nearly as dilapidated as the bus station!) After using the rest room, she spent a half hour persuading the prune-faced landlady to rent her the only remaining bachelor apartment by the week (it was all Kara could afford, but she didn't admit that). The woman—a short, dumpy, doughy matron in a faded housecoat—kept eyeing Kara suspiciously when she avoided the subject of her previous address. What address could she possibly give . . . her beloved, burned-out house? the hospital? her aunt's home? None seemed quite appropriate. But neither could she admit that she had no previous address. Finally, to quell the manager's misgivings, Kara scribbled down her former residence, ironically now a vacant lot boasting the charred rubble of three lives.

Minutes later, Kara stood inside her new abode—a cramped, dreary, uninviting room with a sagging bed on one side and a tiny kitchenette on the other. One small window with torn curtains and an outdated calendar broke the barrenness of gray, soiled walls. A few pieces of shabby, overstuffed furniture were placed at awkward angles, offering little promise of comfort or repose.

But Kara was too exhausted to complain. She collapsed fully dressed on the faded bedspread and slept soundly until noon. Then she got up, freshened her makeup, combed her hair, and began her pursuit for a job in earnest.

She took a bus across town to the Hilltop House, advertised as one of Claremont's most impressive restaurants. Might as well start at the top, she figured. The tight-lipped manager eyed her coolly when she told him she had come to apply for the waitress position. With obvious disdain he handed her the application and nodded toward a back room where she could sit down and write.

When she had completed the application, Kara turned around to look for the manager. Instead, her eyes rested upon a huge lumberjack of a man standing just behind her.

"Hello," he said in a deep, resonant voice.

In a glance Kara took in his brawny good looks—the wheat-colored hair falling casually over his high, tanned forehead, his thick brows shadowing inscrutable, blue-gray eyes, and a long, full nose and wide, chiseled, sensual mouth.

"Hello," Kara replied a bit breathlessly.

"You're applying for a position with us?"

"Yes, I am," said Kara.

He picked up her application and skimmed it. Kara watched him intently. He was wearing a casual navy blue shirt open at the neck, revealing a bronzed, hairy chest. He wore a gold chain around his neck with a curious gold medallion that he fingered unthinkingly as he read.

After a moment he handed the form back to her. Without a word he took a pack of cigarettes from his pocket, removed one, and placed it between his lips. "Kara . . . Kara Strickland," he mused, igniting his lighter and touching the flame to the long white taper. He drew in a breath and exhaled slowly, deliberately.

Kara waited, feeling a keen, painful anticipation. Who was this man? By his suave, take-charge manner he was clearly someone with authority.

"You've had no experience, Miss Strickland."

"What?"

"Experience. According to your application, you've had no previous experience as a waitress."

"I just graduated from high school this past June," Kara explained lamely. "I—I've never had to work before."

"Well, we hire only well-trained girls. Our customers expect prompt, classy service." His eyes narrowed with a calm, smoldering scrutiny. "You have the class all right, but not the background."

Kara felt her face coloring with embarrassment. "I—I never should have come here," she murmured. She picked up her purse and turned to go.

"Hold on, little lady," said the man, putting a restraining hand on her shoulder.

Kara glanced in surprise at the strong hand gripping her, then cautiously met the man's gaze. He promptly released her. His lips curled into a mildly amused grin. Kara noticed the shadow of a beard beneath his freshly shaven skin.

"Let's not be in such a hurry," he told her. He crushed his cigarette in a nearby ashtray and shook her hand amiably.

"Perhaps I should explain. I'm Al Price. This is my place."

"Your place?"

"Yeah, all mine. I'm sorry I can't hire you, but you look like a nice kid. Why don't you give me your phone number, and if anything turns up, I'll call you."

"It's in the application," said Kara in a small, discouraged voice. "That's the hall phone in my apartment building. I don't have one yet."

They said goodbye then. Briefly. Pleasantly. Kara took the bus home. (Incredibly ironic that she already thought of that dismal, suffocating box as "home.") She sat silently in a back seat staring out the bus window. Her spirits were heavy with the weight of disappointment. *It'll always be this way,* she thought sullenly. *I'm not qualified to do anything*.

Kara felt too depressed to return immediately to her apartment, so until dusk she walked around the cluttered shopping area in the vicinity of her new "home," browsing in the dark little shops, gazing absently into dusty store windows. With her few remaining dollars she purchased some fruit and vegetables, a pound of hamburger, paper plates and plastic silverware, a couple of cheap aluminum pans and some cleaning supplies.

Not exactly a splashy way to set up housekeeping, she reflected as she balanced her purchases in one arm and fumbled with the door key. Once inside her apartment, she felt along the wall for the light switch. The plain overhead bulb flooded the room with stark, bluish light. Blinking, Kara looked down, then stifled a scream as several brown, shiny cockroaches scurried for cover.

Weak and trembling, Kara dropped her purchases on the little formica table. She cringed involuntarily, thinking of those terrible, tiny intruders hidden and waiting in the dark recesses of her room. They reminded her chillingly of the sinister old man who had followed her early this morning. They were all waiting in the shadows, invisible by day, but patiently, silently waiting for her to crumble, to give up the fragile personhood she was trying so desperately to reconstruct. But she wouldn't surrender. She wouldn't give them (and now she was thinking of more than the old man and the insects) the satisfaction of seeing her fail.

Under her breath she vowed, "First thing in the morning I'm going to scrub this place from top to bottom with disinfectant!"

9

*T*he next morning, Kara had just finished scouring her apartment when she received a telephone call from Al Price.

"I found you a job, Miss Strickland . . . Kara," he said lightly, with a hint of smugness.

"A job? What . . . where?" she asked in surprise, standing in the semidark hall, wiping her sudsy hands on her jeans.

"It's a little restaurant just off Bloomfield, not far from your place. It's called the Hamburger Hamlet. Nothing fancy, but it's a start, a place where you can learn the business."

"A waitress job—?"

"Right. I set it up with this buddy of mine who runs the place. You can begin tomorrow."

"Tomorrow? That's—that's wonderful!"

"Okay, are you ready for the address—?"

"Wait. Let me get paper and pencil," Kara cried breathlessly. She hesitated, then said out of a sudden wariness, "But first tell me, Mr. Price, why would you do this for me, a total stranger?"

"Call me Al, okay?" he said persuasively. "And let's say I get a kick out of helping people. It's a little hobby of mine."

"Well, I—I don't know how to thank you," said Kara gratefully.

She spent the rest of the day anticipating her new job. Surely it would be hard work, with long, strenuous hours, but she would be earning her own money. That was something she had never done before in her life.

Kara rose early the next morning, showered, washed and styled her hair, applied a tasteful amount of makeup, and put on black slacks and an attractive off-white shirt Aunt Kate had given her (long-sleeved, of course, to cover her still-disfigured arms). She arrived at the restaurant well before eight, smiling and enthusiastic. But before the day was over, she realized that she had underestimated the toil and drudgery of her new position. After eight hours of clearing tables, taking orders, and carrying precariously balanced trays, she knew that she had not regained her strength since her hospital stay. Of course, she had never been physically strong, but neither was she a weakling. She had always depended simply on brain, not brawn, to see her through any difficult situation. Somehow, she had told herself fiercely, she would endure this day—and every long, wearisome day hereafter!

It was dark when Kara finally arrived back at her apartment. She felt exhausted, near collapse. If she could just stumble into bed, she might survive. At least she had grabbed a bite to eat at the restaurant, so she wouldn't have to fix dinner.

As she opened her door, she was surprised to see the light on. Had she left it burning all day? Then her surprise turned to disbelief. Al Price was sitting comfortably on her sofa!

"Hello, little lady," he said, offering a smooth, insinuating smile. "It's about time you got home."

Kara closed the door and put her purse on the table. She tried to keep her voice steady as she said, "What are you doing here, Mr. Price?"

"Please, it's Al," he corrected. "And I'm just checking to see how you liked your new job."

"I like it fine . . . Al. I mean, it's not easy, but I think I'm going to work out all right."

"Good. That's what I like to hear."

She glanced anxiously around the room. "How did you get in here? The door was locked."

"Your landlady," he said offhandedly, sitting back and putting his hands behind his head.

"But how? She wouldn't let you in just like that."

"I told her I was your brother."

"My—my brother?"

Al chuckled to himself. "Yeah. Your long-lost brother Clyde from Cincinnati."

Kara didn't know whether to laugh or cry. "I—I don't understand this—your coming here. Why—?"

He stood up and smoothed his pant legs with a deliberate motion. He was wearing a maroon open-neck shirt and the same gold pendant he had worn previously. He came over and gazed down at Kara with cool, penetrating eyes. "There's something about you that intrigues me," he said in a softly beguiling voice, running his hand over her sleeve.

She stepped back, her heart racing with alarm. "Mr. Price—Al—you'd better go—"

A frown creased his brow. "Go? No. We'll both go. I came here to take you to dinner. We'll celebrate your new job."

"I can't," protested Kara. She couldn't admit that he frightened her. "I'm dead tired," she explained plaintively. "I couldn't possibly go anywhere tonight."

Al's lips tightened in a sneer of displeasure. He ran his fingers through his thick, straw-colored hair, then grunted, "Okay, we'll forget tonight. But I'll pick you up at your work tomorrow night."

Kara stared incredulously at him. "Why are you doing this . . . giving me this . . . this ultimatum?"

He nudged Kara's chin playfully. "Here's something you'd better learn, duchess. When Al Price does something nice, his girls always know how to show their appreciation. You understand?" He sauntered limberly to the door and opened it. Before Kara could think of a reply, he was gone.

———

The next day she fretted through her eight long hours of work. The jammed counters and demanding customers didn't faze her. Even her nearly overwhelming weariness took second place in her thoughts. One person loomed in her mind, a vaguely insidious presence. Al Price. Kara was afraid to go out with him tonight, and yet afraid not to.

She realized the choice had already been made for her when, after work, she spotted Al Price waiting by the cashier's counter. Seeing her, Al smiled and gave a brief, friendly wave. Somehow he didn't look so threatening now. Kara walked over, chiding herself for building him up in her mind as some kind of ogre.

"Hungry, little lady?" he asked pleasantly.

"Starved," she admitted. "Are we going to the Hilltop House?"

"No, I can eat there anytime." He clasped her elbow. "I'm taking you to the only authentic Mexican restaurant in town. They have *camarones zacatecas* that are *magnífico*," he said, putting his fingertips to his lips in a gesture of hearty approval.

"What's that?" asked Kara.

He looked at her in mock surprise. "You don't know? Well, it's a shrimp dish."

"Sounds good to me," she said. "I'll just go change out of my uniform and be right back."

The Acapulco restaurant was only a fifteen-minute drive. A sprawling Spanish-style building, it contained a dozen cozy nooks adorned with an abundance of Mexican relics and mementos. A trio of brightly dressed mariachis strolled among the tables, strumming Spanish guitars, serenading the guests. Kara was enchanted.

When a handsome young man in Mexican garb came to take their order, Al said, "*Tecate, por favor* . . . with a little lime and salt." He answered Kara's questioning glance with, "Tecate is Mexican beer. Want one?"

"No thanks. I think I'll just have a lime soda."

"Have you decided what you want from the menu?" asked Al.

"Yes. I'll have the *tostada compuesta*," she said, struggling with the pronunciation.

"And I'll have the *camarones zacatecas*," said Al, "and put a wedge of avocado on the side."

"*Muy bien, señor*," said the waiter with a slight bow.

"You know a lot about food, don't you?" remarked Kara, dipping a nacho chip into the red-hot salsa.

"I should," replied Al. "I own my own restaurant, remember?"

"Yes, of course. But I was just wondering how you got into it—the restaurant business, I mean."

"My old man was a cook," Al told her, his voice sounding vaguely scornful. "Not a chef, mind you. A cook. He worked his fool head off and never had a dime to show for it. Still doesn't. He's retired now and broke. But, would you believe, he had the gall to nag *me* about being lazy!"

"I'm sorry," said Kara, not quite sure how to reply.

"Just because I wouldn't kiss the feet of some blasted employer! I wasn't about to follow in Pop's footsteps, getting stamped on day after day, inch by inch like a worm."

"So what did you do?"

"I played the angles and got my own restaurant. And before I'm through I'll have a whole string of places. I wonder what my old man will say then?"

"I'm sure he'll be very proud of you."

"Proud?" snarled Al, his eyes narrowing to malevolent slits. "I doubt it. He's too stubborn to admit I could do something on my own, something a whole lot more impressive than he ever did."

When they had finished eating, Al was still talking

grandly about his plans for his chain of restaurants. Finally he sat back, a cigarette between his lips, and eyed Kara curiously. "You think I'm crazy, don't you—or at least unrealistic in my expectations?"

"No, not exactly," said Kara. "I think you're marvelously ambitious. I suppose that's what it takes to get big things done."

"How about you?" he asked, snuffing out his cigarette. "What's your big ambition, your lifelong dream?"

Kara averted her eyes and mumbled, "I have no dreams. At this point in my life I'm not sure . . . who I am."

"Does it have something to do with your scars?" he asked matter-of-factly.

Kara instinctively put her hands in her lap. "My scars?"

"Yes. I noticed your hands. And you seem to wear only long-sleeve, high-neck shirts. I don't suppose it's merely modesty. Was the fire recent?"

"Yes, but I—I can't talk about it." She looked imploringly at him. "I'm awfully tired, Al. I really should get home."

He nodded and signaled for the check. "Whatever you say, duchess."

Al drove Kara back to her apartment and insisted on seeing her inside. "You should get out of this dump," he said, taking the key from her hand and unlocking the door.

"I will when I can afford it." She stepped inside and flipped on the light switch. Then she turned to Al and extended her hand. "I had a nice time tonight, Al. Thank you."

He followed her in and closed the door behind him. Taking her hand, he said, "The night isn't over yet, duchess."

Kara attempted to retrieve her hand, but Al held it firmly. "Please, Al," she pleaded, "I'm very tired. Please go."

"That's funny," he said with a raw chuckle. "I'm just beginning to feel wide awake." Without warning he pulled her against him and kissed her roughly, insistently.

She struggled without success to free herself. At last she managed to gasp, "Let me go, or I'll call the police!"

Al released her and shoved her brusquely away from him. She fell backward onto the couch. "You're a real smart mouth," he said angrily, looming over her. He reached down and cupped her face in one large hand. "You're a real cold fish, aren't you, duchess? Didn't that fire do anything to warm you up?" His fingers pressed more deeply, painfully against her jaw. "I could teach you a lesson right now, lady, a lesson you'd never forget."

"Get out of here!" Kara demanded, wrenching free and scrambling to her feet.

"That's more like it," Al grunted approvingly. "I like my girls full of spice and fire."

"I'm not one of your girls, and I never will be!" Kara cried breathlessly, darting to the door and flinging it open. "Now get out!"

Cursing under his breath, Al Price stalked outside. He took one last backward glance. Glowering menacingly, he warned, "You'll be sorry, little lady. Just wait. You'll be sorry you crossed Al Price."

With a sudden surge of energy, Kara slammed the door in his face and hastily locked it. Outraged, Al kicked the door vehemently. Again . . . and again! Hysterically, Kara envisioned the frail door exploding open and Al Price coming at her, insane with rage. Would he murder her, or would he—? No, it was unthinkable!

She realized suddenly that the hideous pounding and clatter had stopped. She waited, scarcely breathing. Two minutes . . . three . . . five. Thank God, there was only blessed, welcome silence. Relief washed over her.

Kara sank limply to the floor and began to sob.

10

Kara couldn't sleep all night. Her muscles were tense; her back ached. She must have wrenched it when Al shoved her against the couch. Her mouth was also sore from his savage kiss. Every time she began to doze, she saw Al Price hovering over her, poised to attack. It was ironic that her nightly, macabre dreams of the fire should be replaced by an equally terrifying specter, the abominable Al Price. Even more ironic, because the fire no longer posed a threat, while Al Price presented a genuine, ongoing danger.

Around three a.m. Kara got up and fixed herself some hot tea. (Her boss, taking pity on her sorry financial state, had sent her home with extra packets of tea, coffee, sugar, and cream.)

Kara sat on her bed in the semidarkness sipping tea, her legs drawn up under her so that cockroaches wouldn't run across her bare feet. Earlier she had cried herself to sleep, but the sleep hadn't lasted long. There had been only the dozing, then the dreams, followed by stark wakefulness.

Now, in these eerie predawn hours, Kara could no longer cry. Nor could she escape her terrors, her memories, or her pain. For the first time in several days she cautiously permitted herself to think about her mother—or mothers. Anna and Catherine. Catherine and Anna. Who was really her mother— the woman who bore her or the woman who raised her? The question was too intolerable to consider, the truth still too abhorrent to confront.

74

"If only Dad were here," Kara said yearningly. "He'd know what to do." Truly, Ben Strickland had always had the answers for Kara. When she was a child, she had depended on him unquestioningly, without hesitation. If only she could turn to him now.

"Why did you have to die, Daddy?" she whispered despairingly. "Why! Why did you go out that night when you were already safe at home? What made you leave so suddenly, without a word?"

A remote, unexplored thought struck her then, leaving her breathless, stunned. If Anna is not my mother, then Ben Strickland is not my father! How could she possibly have overlooked that fact? So obvious, so nakedly apparent! Yet, in her shock and anger, she had missed it, had not once entertained the idea. If anything, this new fact was more dismaying than the knowledge that Anna was not her natural mother. Anna, in a peculiar, undefined way, had never seemed quite comfortable in her role as mother. But Ben, her beloved father! Surely he had cherished her as deeply as any parent could.

Or did he, in some mysterious way, love and accept her, not for herself alone, but because she was Catherine Hardin's daughter? Impossible. Unthinkable!

Or was it?

Another startling thought took shape. *Who then is my father and where is he now?*

Finished with her tea, Kara stood up, her mind absorbed with questions. She listened to the sounds of the night—the muted blast of a car horn, the constant gnawing of mice in the woodwork, the distant, steady whir of tires on dew-wet pavement. But her own thoughts rang louder, sharper, more insistent.

"I have another father," she mused aloud, in awe. "Maybe he's still alive. Maybe he's out there somewhere wondering about me, waiting for me to find him. Who is he?

What is he like? How can I find him?"

Of course! Aunt Kate. Catherine. She would know. Kara, in spite of her animosity, would go and ask her, demand an answer. At this moment it was the most important question in Kara's life.

––––––––

The next day, after work, Kara took the bus to Aunt Kate's neighborhood, then walked the six blocks to her house. She arrived at twilight and knocked soundly on the door. A minute later Kate greeted her with a look of astonishment.

"Kara! I didn't expect to see you—"

"I know. I wouldn't have come, but I—I need to talk to you."

Catherine stepped aside and said kindly, "Come in, Kara, please. Can I get you something, some tea or a glass of juice?"

"Nothing," replied Kara. She sat down formally on the sofa.

Kate sat across from her. "I've been worried about you, dear. I didn't know where you'd gone, and I knew you didn't have much money."

"I'm all right. I have a job and an apartment." *No sense in adding any of the grim details to give Aunt Kate a reason to gloat or say I-told-you-so.*

"A job and an apartment? Already?" Kate asked in surprise.

"I guess I was lucky." Kara shrugged, then looked questioningly at Kate. "How is Anna? Have you heard anything?"

"I talked to Dr. Lasky yesterday on the phone. He said there's little change. He's hoping to be able to start skin-grafting procedures in a week or so."

"I guess that'll be a long, painful process," reflected Kara somberly.

"Yes, I'm afraid so," Kate agreed. "When do you plan to go see her again?"

Kara shifted uncomfortably. "I don't know. Not for a while. I—I just can't face her right now . . . knowing what I know."

Catherine nodded.

Kara rubbed her hands together nervously. "What I came here for, Aunt Kate—I mean—" She paused, flustered, then exclaimed, "I don't even know what to call you now!"

"Call me simply Kate . . . or Catherine."

"All right . . . Catherine. The reason I came here was to find out who my—my father is. My natural father."

"Your father?" Kate stood up and walked to the window. Absently she straightened a section of the luxuriant, pale green drapes. "Your father has always been Ben Strickland," she told Kara. "He adored you as if you were his own child. Isn't that enough?"

"No, it isn't," returned Kara sharply. "I want to know about the man who . . . who gave me life."

Kate turned and gazed soberly at Kara. "I told you about him—"

"I want his name."

"I can't tell you that."

"Why not? Surely you haven't forgotten."

A wounded expression flickered in Catherine's eyes. "He doesn't know you exist, Kara. He never even knew I was pregnant. It would do no one any good for you to know his name."

Kara stood up and approached Kate, eyeing her directly. "I have a right to know. All of you have made my life a lie. I can't pick up the pieces until I know the whole truth."

Catherine shook her head ponderously. "Oh, Kara, I know you have a right to the truth, but this man—he has long since forgotten me. He has his own life—a very successful one—and a family. They're very happy. I don't want to do anything to upset that."

"You won't," said Kara urgently. "I wouldn't tell his family. I don't want to hurt anyone. I just want to know who he is, what he's like. He represents half of my heritage, my history. I need to know about him."

"Someday," responded Kate. "When the time is right, when you have had time to see things in perspective, then I'll tell you."

"That's not good enough," retorted Kara. "If you don't tell me now, I'll find someone who will. I won't stop looking until I find him. And I won't care then who knows the truth!"

"Surely you don't mean that."

"I've never been more serious."

After several moments, Catherine reached out and gently touched Kara's arm. "Your father's name is Wilson Seyers."

"Wilson Seyers?" repeated Kara slowly, marveling over the sound of it. She looked closely at Kate and asked, "Who is he? Where can I find him?"

"You said you wouldn't—tell him!" exclaimed Catherine.

"I said I wouldn't tell his family."

"You can't do this, Kara. You can't destroy his life."

Kara stared in amazement at Kate. "You're still in love with him, aren't you, after all these years!"

"That's not important," replied Kate. "Enough people have suffered because of my mistake. I can't add any more."

"Does he live in this state? In this city? Where?"

"Kara, you mustn't—!"

"He lives here, doesn't he, in this very city?"

"Yes."

"Where?"

"I don't know the address."

"That's all right. It shouldn't be hard to find in the telephone book."

"Don't go to his home," Kate begged. "There's another way to reach him."

"How?"

"Will . . . Wilson is the editor of the *Claremont News*, our local paper."

11

*T*he Claremont newspaper offices were located in an old brick building on Main Street in the center of town. Kara went there the very next morning, in spite of the fact that she would be putting her job at the Hamburger Hamlet in jeopardy by arriving late. Regardless of the consequences, she had to meet this man Wilson Seyers, her father. If she put off the confrontation, she might lose her courage.

She wended her way through the newsroom and outer offices, striding with a brisk, purposeful air, hoping no one would inquire why she was there. Escaping the pungent smells of newsprint, ink, and machinery, she reached the inner offices, where the carpet was plush and the walls richly paneled with mahogany. Only one last barrier to pass—the editor's private secretary, a small, blond woman in a tailored suit. Looking up curiously as Kara approached her desk, she said pleasantly, "Good morning. May I help you?"

"Hello," said Kara, trying to sound casual and confident. "I'd like to see Mr. Seyers, please."

"Do you have an appointment?"

"Not exactly," admitted Kara. "But I must see Mr. Seyers. It's urgent."

"Is it a business matter?"

"No. It's—it's personal."

"Very well. Let me ask if he will see you." The woman pushed a button on the intercom and a man's voice responded. "Yes, Ruth, what is it?"

"There's someone here to see you, Mr. Seyers. She doesn't have an appointment, but she says it's important."

"What's her name?"

"Kara . . . Kara Strickland," said Kara quickly.

The secretary repeated the name and the deep, husky voice returned with, "Kara Strickland? Never heard of her. What does she want?"

"She says it's personal."

There was a pause, then the voice replied abruptly, "Tell her I'll give her a minute."

The woman looked up at Kara and said, "He'll see you, but please remember he's very busy. You'll have to keep it brief."

"Thank you," said Kara, catching her breath. She had made it! In a moment, for the first time in her life, she would gaze into the face of her real father. She felt a momentary pinch of guilt that she could actually consider another man her father. She would never betray the memory of Ben Strickland, but neither could she ignore the implications that came with the knowledge of her natural father's existence.

"You may go in now, Miss Strickland," said the secretary, breaking into Kara's thoughts.

Kara nodded and walked gingerly through the door marked CITY EDITOR. Her eyes focused on a man sitting behind a large, cluttered desk. He was of medium build and had thinning, auburn-blond hair. Gray eyes accented a pleasant, ruddy face. His features were not striking, nor especially familiar. Kara was faintly disappointed that she felt no deep, instinctive response to this man who played so crucial a role in her life.

"You wanted to see me, Miss . . . Miss—?"

"Strickland. Kara. Yes, I—I—" The words, so carefully arranged in her mind, had suddenly evaporated. Her throat constricted. Her mouth went dry.

"Kara, you say?" he mused. "That's an unusual name.

It so happens that was my grandmother's name."

"Really?" murmured Kara with interest.

"Would you like to sit down?" He gestured toward a nearby chair.

"Thank you," said Kara with relief, gratefully taking the chair.

"I suppose you came for a job," observed Mr. Seyers, lightly tapping a pencil on his desk.

"A job? No. It's—another matter."

"Really? I would have guessed you were a journalism major at City College."

"No, although I do like to write. Last year I was editor of my high school paper. But I prefer poetry . . . literary things."

Mr. Seyers cleared his throat impatiently. "Miss Strickland, I'm sorry. We rarely use poetry in our paper, and I really don't have time just for chitchat."

"I understand that," replied Kara, duly chastened. "It's just that this is very hard for me to say."

Leaning forward slightly, he asked, "What is hard for you to say?"

"I just found out myself," she rushed on nervously. "Last night, in fact. It's been a shock for me, learning the truth in bits and pieces—"

The editor tapped his pencil more vigorously. "What truth, Miss Strickland? So far you've talked only in riddles."

"I'm sorry, Mr. Seyers. I'm afraid I'm handling this very poorly." Kara forced her eyes to meet his squarely. "I came here to tell you that . . . I am . . . your daughter."

The pencil tapping stopped. He stared at her incredulously. "This is either a very poor joke, or you must be out of your mind, young lady," he said severely.

"No, it's true," protested Kara. "You are my father."

Wilson Seyers broke his pencil in half in a gesture of barely suppressed rage. "I see your little game, Miss Strickland, and it won't work. Get out of here before I call the police."

Kara's mouth quivered involuntarily as she exclaimed, "A game? Is that what you think this is? Believe me, this is no more pleasant for me than it is for you!"

Seyers stood up and leaned across his desk toward her. "Let me make it perfectly clear to you," he said, his voice edged with contempt, "I have one daughter and one son. That is all. Now if you'll excuse me, I'm a very busy man."

Kara clutched the arms of her chair. "I have no intention of leaving, Mr. Seyers. Not until you've heard me out."

His expression revealed a man struggling to regain his composure and assuage his anger. Finally, his voice steadying, he replied, "Very well. But speak quickly. Then go!"

Kara cleared her throat and said boldly, "I found out only recently that my parents—the couple I thought were my parents—adopted me. My real mother is my aunt. She wasn't married and didn't feel she could keep me."

"And just who is your mother?" inquired Wilson Seyers skeptically.

"Catherine Hardin."

Seyers' face turned ashen. His eyes clouded, registering a mixture of shock, disbelief, and anger. "How dare you—!"

"It's true," said Kara firmly. "Catherine loved you very much. But then you went off and married someone else."

For a few moments Seyers' face softened as he apparently recalled faint, fragile memories. "Catherine . . ." he murmured, his eyes moving to a spot beyond Kara. But his reverie shattered as he realized Kara was watching him shrewdly. Immediately he was on the defensive again. "This is ridiculous!" he stormed. "Catherine would have told me if she was pregnant."

"No, she wouldn't. She didn't, because you had already married someone else," Kara reminded him. "She didn't want to interfere with your happiness."

The intercom buzzed then. Seyers jabbed the button impatiently and snapped, "Ruth, hold all my calls. I can't be disturbed now." Looking back at Kara, he tugged at his tie that already hung loose and slightly askew. He walked around his desk to the window and stared out morosely. After a long moment he turned to Kara and studied her with suspicion. "Just supposing what you say is true—and I'm not for a minute conceding that it is—but just supposing, what do you want out of all this? What's your angle?"

Kara looked at him, perplexed. "I don't understand. What do you mean—angle?"

"You know doggone well what I mean," he exploded. "What are you after—money?"

"No, I don't want your money!" cried Kara indignantly.

"Then what? You must have come here expecting something."

Kara clasped her arms around her waist, almost a protective gesture, and shook her head. She was afraid she might begin to cry. "I don't know what I expected," she told him shakily. "I didn't think that far ahead. I just knew I had to see you." She gazed earnestly at him. "All the time I was growing up, my life was very happy and complete. But this year some things happened—terrible things—and I discovered my life was filled with huge, gaping holes. All the things I had taken for granted were suddenly big question marks. Or worse—lies! Now I'm trying to find out who I really am. I figure somebody somewhere knows me and will help me put the pieces together."

"I'm afraid, in this case, Miss Strickland, you've come to the wrong man."

Kara choked out the words, "Are you saying you're not my father?"

Seyers stepped toward her, his eyes coldly determined. "What I'm saying is that it doesn't matter. I already have a family and a good, successful life. There's no room in it for you or anyone else. I suggest you go back to wherever you came from and forget you ever heard the name Wilson Seyers."

In spite of herself Kara began to cry. "I came here to meet my father," she blurted, fighting back her tears, "and instead, all I've met is a cruel stranger!" She turned and fled blindly out of his office.

As she hurried self-consciously past Mr. Seyers' secretary, Kara collided with someone entering the office—a girl about Kara's age. The two collected themselves and laughed with embarrassment.

"I'm so sorry," said the girl, touching Kara's arm apologetically.

"No, it's my fault," insisted Kara. "I wasn't watching where I was going."

The girl looked more closely at her. "You're crying. Is there anything I can do to help?"

Kara shook her head and started to step around the girl.

But the girl was persistent. "Did Mr. Seyers say something to upset you?"

Kara nodded and tried again to make her escape. "Were you seeing him about a job?"

"Yes—a job," Kara replied distractedly, anxious to get away.

"Well, certainly my father could have let you down a little easier than this," remarked the girl with a note of disapproval.

Kara stared in surprise and curiosity at the girl, suddenly aware that here stood her very own half sister. Incredible! It hadn't as yet sunk in that Mr. Seyers' children were her own brother and sister. What a marvelous realization! Kara had always regretted being an only child. "You're Mr. Seyers' daughter?" she questioned with undisguised interest.

"Yes, and I apologize for my father. Sometimes he can be a bit gruff, but he's very nice underneath." The girl smiled warmly. She had a round, pretty face with delicate features and chestnut hair waving back in loose, casual curls.

Kara smiled faintly. "It was my fault anyway. I should have known better than to expect a job when I've had no real training."

"Listen," said the girl, brightening. "I just have to drop off some papers my father left at home, then I'll be on my way to summer school. But I have about an hour before class if you'd like to go have something to eat. Have you had breakfast yet?"

"No, but I don't know—" said Kara uncertainly.

"Please. I feel sort of responsible for your distress, since it was my father who upset you. Maybe if we sit down and talk you'll feel better. Perhaps we could even come up with another job lead for you."

"All right," decided Kara, beginning to relish the idea. Even if her father wouldn't accept her, surely there was no harm in getting acquainted with her new sister. In fact, it struck Kara as a rather daring, appealing thing to do. "Where shall we go?" she asked eagerly.

"There's a pancake house next door. I eat breakfast there sometimes. They have great buttermilk pancakes." The girl paused to greet her father's secretary and deliver the folder, then she and Kara were on their way.

As they walked down the hall together and out the front entrance, Kara smiled and said, "We haven't even introduced ourselves. My name is Kara Strickland."

"And I'm Carrie Seyers," said the girl. "Actually my father named me Catherine and my mother nicknamed me Carrie."

Kara looked over quickly but realized with relief that "Catherine" had no special significance for Carrie beyond her own name. But it was noteworthy that Wilson Seyers had selected that particular name for his daughter.

The two girls spent the next half hour talking together

over steaming stacks of pancakes. Kara, very nearly broke, was relieved that Carrie insisted on treating.

"You're not from Claremont, are you?" observed Carrie, pouring more syrup onto her pancakes.

"No. I'm from Westchester." Kara went on to explain briefly about her father's death and the fire that had devastated their home and incapacitated her mother. She carefully avoided the issue of her true parentage. Finally she concluded, "So I came to Claremont to stay with my aunt, but we don't get along too well, so last week I moved into my own place."

"And now you need a job," said Carrie sympathetically.

"Well, I have a job as a waitress at the Hamburger Hamlet, but it's not the sort of thing I want to do permanently."

"Have you studied journalism?"

"A little in high school. I graduated this past June."

"Well, why don't you take some night courses at City College this fall," suggested Carrie. "One of the writing instructors is a friend of mine. His name is Greg Arlen. He's really terrific."

"Maybe I'll do that," said Kara. "I've always liked to write."

"Really? Me too," marveled Carrie. "Of course, I've limited most of my writing to my diary and a few poems."

"So have I," chuckled Kara. "Most of them I wouldn't show anybody! But I am a bit proud of the articles I did for my school paper."

"We have quite a lot in common," noted Carrie, pleased. "In the fall I'll be senior editor of my high school yearbook."

"That's great." Kara studied Carrie thoughtfully. "You must be—what?—about seventeen?"

"Yes. Just last month. How about you?"

"Eighteen last April."

After finishing her last bite, Carrie glanced at her watch

and exclaimed, "Oh, goodness, I've got to run. I'll be late for class!" She stood up and smiled at Kara. "Let's do this again sometime, okay?"

"I'd love to," Kara replied sincerely.

"I have a wonderful idea," said Carrie, suddenly beaming. "Why don't you come over for dinner tomorrow evening? We can continue our conversation then."

Kara's mouth dropped open in surprise. "You want me to come to your house? For dinner?"

"Sure. Why not?" said Carrie, scribbling her address on a napkin. "Make it about seven, okay?"

"Won't your folks mind—I mean, a stranger coming to dinner?"

"Oh, no. They encourage me to bring home my friends. I have a super family. Just wait'll you meet them. Even my little brother's not so bad once you get to know him." Carrie laughed lightly. "And you've already met my dad, of course, but you'll like him much better when he's not all business. So how about it? Will you come?"

Kara heaved a sigh of indecision and whistled low through her teeth. Then she looked at Carrie and found herself nodding. "I'd love to come!" she said giddily. "In fact, I don't know when I've looked forward to anything more!"

As Carrie strode away from the table, Kara sat back and mused with a mixture of smugness and trepidation. *Well, Mr. Wilson Seyers, guess who's coming to dinner!*

12

$\mathcal{T}$he Seyers home was a sprawling ranch-style house on a generous fenced lot in a suburb of Claremont. The grass was a brilliant green, as thick as a carpet, and neatly trimmed. The trees and shrubs surrounding the house formed a striking design, creating a picture-postcard aura.

Kara arrived just before seven. The bus had brought her to within a mile of the house. She hadn't minded the brisk, invigorating walk through such a plush neighborhood. But now her breath was scant—whether from the walk or from nervousness, she wasn't sure. She had no idea what sort of reception she would receive from Wilson Seyers. Would he pretend they had never met, or would he explode in anger and throw her bodily out of his house? No doubt he would consider her a threat—his unknown, unclaimed daughter. Somehow she would have to reassure him that she had no intention of revealing the truth of his paternity to his wife and children. All she wanted was an opportunity to become acquainted with her newfound family. She would make no claims, no demands, no trouble. But would Wilson understand that her motives were pure (or at least not malicious)?

I'll find out soon enough, she reflected soberly as she pressed the doorbell. Carrie, in a bright coral sweater and jeans, her face rosy in the twilight, greeted Kara with a warm, receptive smile. "Hello, Kara. I'm so glad you came. Come on in!"

The house was tastefully decorated with colonial furniture—solid oak tables and comfortable, flower-print chairs. It was a warm, inviting atmosphere. Kara felt immediately at home—until she came face-to-face with Wilson Seyers. She could tell by his astonished expression that he hadn't expected to see her again. Certainly not tonight in his own home, the eagerly anticipated guest of his daughter.

He stared silently at her as Carrie made the introductions. "You remember Kara, don't you, Daddy? She was in your office yesterday."

"I remember," he said tight-lipped, his eyes boring into Kara's.

Kara, shifting from one foot to the other, looked away uncomfortably. Her gaze focused on an attractive woman with shoulder-length, golden brown hair entering the living room. She flashed a welcoming smile. "You must be Kara, Carrie's new friend," she said pleasantly. "I'm Lynn Seyers, Carrie's mother."

Kara nodded and returned the greetings, glad to escape Wilson Seyers' steel-cold glare.

"We met yesterday at Daddy's office," Carrie explained in a light, bubbly rush of words. "Kara was looking for a job, but Daddy was a meany and wouldn't give her one."

"A job—?" her father repeated uncomprehendingly.

Carrie gave him an impetuous hug. "Oh, Daddy, don't look so dour. I'm only kidding. You're no meany. And Kara understands now that she needs the proper training to work in a newspaper office."

"That's right," said Kara quickly, furtively signaling Seyers with her eyes. "I never should have come to your office yesterday expecting a job when I'm so inexperienced. I understand now why you had to say no."

"Miss Strickland, I'm not at all sure you understand the meaning of no," he said in a low, menacing tone.

"Let's just say I have a better idea today what I can expect and what I can't," she replied.

"I think your expectations are still running dangerously high," he snapped ominously.

Kara turned away. Since her father was refusing to drop this deadly verbal exchange, she decided to simply ignore him.

"Daddy, please," interrupted Carrie. "Let's forget yesterday. It's not important. What's important is that I've met a new friend and I want all of you to get to know her."

"We'll have to continue this discussion around the table," announced Lynn Seyers, nodding toward the dining room. She looked at her husband. "The roast is ready, Will, and you're the expert carver."

Kara took her place at the table beside Carrie. The meal looked delectable—rare roast beef, mashed potatoes and gravy, creamed asparagus, and steaming loaves of sourdough bread. There was one empty place at the table. Kara glanced questioningly at Carrie, and Carrie looked at her mother. "Where's Danny?" she asked.

"In his room, as usual," replied Mrs. Seyers, a tone of weary tolerance in her voice. "Would you go get him, Carrie?"

A minute later Carrie returned to the table with a red-headed boy in his middle teens. "This is my brother, Danny," she said as they sat down.

Danny had a spattering of freckles across his wide, upturned nose and thick brows forming a noticeable arc over crinkling gray eyes. He smiled shyly at Kara and his slightly protruding ears turned pink. But he said nothing. He put his napkin in his lap and reached hungrily for the mashed potatoes.

"Just a minute, Danny," said his mother. "We haven't prayed yet."

"Oh, yeah," he grunted and looked down sheepishly.

Kara's spirits plunged momentarily at the mention of prayer. Surely the affluent, sophisticated Seyers weren't religious fanatics like Aunt Ka—Catherine Hardin!

Mrs. Seyers prayed briefly, but Kara noticed that neither Danny nor Wilson Seyers closed their eyes. She felt meagerly reassured by their expressions of sullen endurance. Praying was apparently a harmless quirk of preference for Mrs. Seyers.

The dinner conversation was a strange mixture of earnest, amiable chitchat, awkward silences, and resentful glances (from Wilson). Carrie and her mother were obviously attempting to put Kara at ease and make her feel at home. But Danny ate in self-absorbed silence, ignoring everyone, while Wilson Seyers remained clearly disgruntled over Kara's presence. He responded with only monosyllabic growls, which obviously baffled and dismayed his wife and daughter.

You're the one who's going to blow this whole thing, Kara wanted to tell him. His behavior was certain to arouse suspicion. Couldn't he see that?

Apparently he could, for by the end of the meal he was actually asking Kara a few random questions in a polite, though subdued voice.

He's fishing for information, Kara figured, but that was all right with her. She wanted him to know all about her. She wanted to leave an unforgettable impression on this strange, fretful man, her father.

While Mrs. Seyers served strawberry shortcake for dessert, Kara gazed with quiet interest around the table, from one person to another. She felt unexpectedly awestruck, dazzled. It seemed impossible that she should be sitting here in this home, sharing a meal with people who were strangers to her and yet blood relatives. Family.

What did the word mean—family? What, if any, was her responsibility to these people and theirs to her? Or did it even matter—for there could be no responsibility assumed where the secret was not known. Their bloodline, that invisible cord that bound her to them forever, could never be divulged. The realization gave Kara a fleeting sense of depression, of hope-lessness.

Shortly after dinner she prepared to leave. No sense in pushing her luck with Wilson Seyers, she decided. "Work to-morrow," she told Mrs. Seyers after thanking her for the din-ner. Work—surely an appropriate and logical excuse.

At the door Carrie asked in surprise, "Where's your car?"

"I don't have one," replied Kara. "I took the bus."

"And you plan to catch one at this time of night?"

Kara nodded. "I checked the schedule. The last one comes by around ten."

"Well, forget the bus," said Carrie emphatically. "I'll drive you home."

There was no dissuading Carrie, and Kara was just as glad. She hadn't been looking forward to that long, lonely bus ride home. The two girls left together in spite of the disap-proving stares of Carrie's father. Kara was pleased to have one last opportunity to talk with Carrie in the congenial privacy of the family car.

"My mom really likes you," Carrie told her as they neared Kara's apartment.

"I like her too. Your whole family is very nice."

Carrie gave her a sidelong glance. "I'm sorry my dad was in such a rotten mood tonight. He must have had a bad day at work."

"That's all right," replied Kara. "I know how that goes."

Carrie smiled. "Thanks for being so understanding."

I understand better than you'll ever know, Kara reflected silently. She felt a sudden yearning to be honest with Carrie, to tell her just who she was. *Carrie, I'm your very own sister. We share the same father.* But no. She didn't dare tell her. She had promised both Catherine Hardin and Wilson Seyers. It was a promise she would have to honor at all costs.

Minutes later, Carrie pulled up in front of the dismal

apartment building that Kara reluctantly called home. As Kara climbed out of the car, Carrie said, "We'll see each other again. I'll call you in a day or so."

"Great," said Kara. Yet she couldn't help but wonder if their paths would indeed cross again. Not if Wilson Seyers had anything to say about it.

The girls said a quick goodbye, and Kara hurried inside the hallway to her door. She still had fleeting, vivid recollections of the old man who had followed her from the bus depot. But thank goodness, the musty, shadowy hallway was empty. Tacked on her door was a note from the landlady. It said, "Your Aunt Kate telephoned. Call ASAP."

Kara crumpled the note in her hand and made her way to the hall telephone. She dialed Kate's number with trembling fingers, fighting a rising fear that something had happened to Anna. When Kate's voice came on the line, Kara blurted, "Is it Anna? Is she all right?"

"Oh, yes, Kara, she's about the same," Catherine assured her. "I'm calling about another matter entirely. Could you come see me this weekend?"

"I—I don't know—"

"It's about your father's will, Kara. I learned today that Ben's estate is out of probate. There are some things we need to discuss."

"Okay. How about noon on Saturday?"

"Fine. I'll have lunch ready, if that's all right with you."

"I guess so. But please don't fuss."

On Saturday Kara arrived at Kate's home promptly at noon, and as she might have guessed, Catherine had fussed. The lunch table was spread with a luscious fruit salad, ham on rye sandwiches, baked beans, and a brimming relish tray.

As they ate, Catherine explained her reason for summoning Kara. "Your family lawyer telephoned me a few days ago because he didn't know where to reach you. He wants you to contact him as soon as possible."

"Why?"

"Because, as I said, your father's estate is out of probate. I don't know the details, but you will be receiving a monthly allowance, plus a generous inheritance when you turn twenty-one."

"I didn't know," murmured Kara in disbelief. "Somehow I thought everything was lost in the fire."

"No. Your father had savings and a number of good investments. I'm not saying you'll never have to work again, but the money should make a good buffer."

"Against poverty?" mused Kara wryly. "That's just what I need right now. Maybe I can get myself a decent place to live."

Catherine smiled. "You're still welcome here, Kara. The door will always be open."

"Thanks, but I can't. I've got to do this on my own."

"It's just that I'm concerned about you—your health . . . your safety."

"I'm doing okay," insisted Kara.

When they had finished eating, Catherine stood up and began to clear the table. She returned a minute later with a plate of sugar cookies and frosty goblets of sherbet. "You loved these cookies when you were little," she told Kara. "You would beg for them for hours."

Kara ignored the reference to her childhood. "I have a feeling you're trying to fatten me up," she said with mock suspicion.

"And I suspect you've forgotten Dr. Lasky's instructions to eat well," returned Kate, mildly scolding her.

"Not so," argued Kara. "In fact, if people keep feeding me so well, I'll probably become a blimp."

"People?" echoed Catherine knowingly. "Or do you mean Wilson Seyers' family?"

Kara looked up in surprise. "How did you know about that?"

"Will came to see me yesterday. He wanted to know about you."

"What did you say?" asked Kara guardedly. She sensed that this uneasy truce with Catherine was about to collapse.

"I told him the truth," replied Kate. "He knows now that you really are his child."

Kara unconsciously stirred her melting sherbet. "How did he react?"

"He was visibly shaken, Kara." Catherine was gathering her words carefully. "He was angry and baffled that I had kept the truth from him all these years. I suppose I had no right to do it."

"Did he say how he felt . . . about me?"

"No, I don't know how he feels, but I could see that he's afraid you will hurt his wife and children."

"I don't want to hurt anyone," argued Kara, her emotions rising.

"Then please, let them be," pleaded Catherine. "Stay out of their lives. Don't hurt them just because you've been hurt."

Kara quietly finished her dessert, knowing intuitively that she could make no such promise. Already in her heart she sensed that she would never be able to leave Wilson Seyers and his family alone. They held the secret to her own identity. If only she could unravel the mystery of their lives, perhaps she could solve the enigma of her own as well. It was an odyssey she would have to pursue, regardless of the consequences.

13

After returning home from her visit with Catherine, Kara spent the evening swatting cockroaches off her bed and out of her cupboards. The nasty little things were multiplying mercilessly, proliferating by leaps and bounds, attacking every meager morsel of food she had in her kitchenette. She vowed that the day she received her first monthly allowance check from her father's estate, she would move into a decent, bug-free apartment.

Even after the cockroaches had been felled and tidily swept away, Kara found herself unable to relax or sleep. Life was moving too fast lately, constantly changing hues, taking on new meanings and facets before she could quite absorb and interpret the previous day's events.

As she thought about it now, she realized that all of her life the people she loved had fit into neat, predictable compartments. She had not had to question how she felt about them nor how they felt about her. She had been safe, secure, confident in her niche as Ben and Anna Strickland's daughter.

But now, knowing the truth, knowing that she was not Ben and Anna's daughter, everything in her life was turned topsy-turvy. No relationship remained simple and uncomplicated. Every person was suspect, his or her motives demanding scrutiny. Even Kara herself was suspect. She could no longer be sure of her own feelings, her underlying motivations.

In the past, before her father's death, she had rarely had

occasion to feel intense anger, hatred, or resentment. But now, over these past few months, her feelings toward everyone seemed tainted by bitterness or suspicion. She resented Anna who had deceived her, pretending for eighteen years to be her mother. Nearly as infuriating was the fact that Anna's weakness had caused the fire that almost destroyed them both. And Kara hated Catherine, the sanctimonious woman who had relinquished her own child and remained a virtual stranger throughout Kara's life. Kara could not even be sure now of her feelings for Ben Strickland, her beloved father, whose death had nearly devastated her. Could she still love unreservedly a man who was not what he claimed to be? Even more crucial, how had Ben really felt about her? As devoted as he had always been, why had he permitted Kara to live a lie?

It occurred to Kara that at the moment there was only one person for whom she felt affection without rancor. That was Carrie Seyers, a sweet, guileless girl, as open and vulnerable as Kara herself had been until this year. But even Kara's friendship with Carrie was based on a lie. How eagerly, she wondered, would Lynn and Carrie Seyers welcome her into their home if they guessed her true identity?

These questions and a hundred more roiled Kara's mind as she waited wearily for sleep to overtake her. She grew increasingly depressed, brooding over the fact that there was no one on earth she could care for with honest, uncluttered devotion.

Finally, wide awake and thoroughly agitated, Kara got up and poured herself a glass of milk. She stood beside the sink and drank by the pale glow of the oven light, refusing to allow her eyes to be assaulted by the harsh glare of the dangling overhead bulb. She was aware of faintly rancid smells emanating from the cupboards and the muted, seemingly omnipresent sounds of insects scurrying along the floor and mice chewing the old building's crusty innards.

"I've got to get out of this hole," she uttered aloud to no one. Automatically her mind argued, *You could be living in Catherine's comfortable home right now if you weren't such a pigheaded fool!*

Abruptly Kara pushed the accusation away and returned to her bed. Still sleepless, she felt a wedge of relief that at least tomorrow was Sunday. She could sleep till noon if she wanted to.

Which she did, yielding herself gratefully to long, sweet hours of exhausted slumber—half the day, at least.

By Monday morning Kara was feeling rested and herself again, in spite of the fact that she faced a brand-new week of toil at the Hamburger Hamlet. The work was hard and the hours long, but at least it kept her mind occupied and gave her something to do, and above all, kept her from the clutches of poverty!

Shortly after Kara arrived home on Monday evening, she received a phone call from Carrie, inviting her to a church picnic on Saturday.

"A church picnic?" Kara echoed dubiously.

"We'll have a great time," Carrie assured her, the words spilling over one another as she added, "There'll be lots of food and hikes and swimming and softball and a huge campfire—"

"Well, I do have this weekend off," said Kara, laughing. At least it wouldn't be like being trapped in a church with a pompous minister saying things that made her feel he was pointing a finger right at her.

"Then you'll go? Wonderful!" cried Carrie. "Greg and I will be by to pick you up at ten sharp."

"Greg?"

"Yes. Greg Arlen. You remember—the guy I told you about. He teaches at City College and he's our church youth director. He's been a friend of our family all of my life. You'll love him!"

On Saturday morning Kara was ready and waiting in front of her apartment building by nine-thirty. There was no way she wanted anyone seeing inside the dank, dreary place she occupied, so better to stand out here, even if she waited an hour.

Just before ten, a sporty metallic blue sedan pulled up beside the curb. Carrie jumped out, and so did a tall, attractive blond in his midtwenties. He had a lean, athletic build and perfectly chiseled features—a full, firm jaw, cleft chin, and deep-set hazel eyes under well-drawn brows. He grinned broadly at Kara.

"This is Greg Arlen," said Carrie, proudly taking his arm as they approached her.

"Hi, Greg," she greeted, feeling an unexpected response—was it shyness, timidity, awe?

"Hi, Kara," he said, taking her hand. His clasp was strong and warm. "Carrie has talked a lot about you. I'm glad you're joining us today."

Kara felt herself blushing. "I'm glad too," she managed.

"Did you bring your swimsuit?" asked Carrie.

Kara's smile faltered. "No, I didn't. I'm not much for swimming." She didn't add that she had no suit and wouldn't have revealed her scarred arms anyway.

"Well, there'll be plenty to do," said Greg cheerfully. "You won't be bored a minute, I promise."

"So let's go," said Carrie, turning back to the car.

That afternoon and evening were unlike anything Kara had experienced before. She had never been one to mingle easily with strangers or to participate in strenuous group sports, but today she found herself doing both. The people were friendly and outgoing, the air was invigorating, and Kara found herself delighting in Carrie and Greg's company. Everyone devoured crispy, black-skinned hot dogs smothered in mustard, baked beans with molasses, and bottles of lemon-lime soda. They hiked, played softball, and swung giddily on the children's swings.

At sunset they rolled up their pant legs and waded along the shallow edge of the lake, frolicking like youngsters. Kara and Carrie teasingly splashed Greg until he threatened to toss them, clothes and all, into the water. Then after dark everyone gathered around the campfire and toasted marshmallows and sang songs.

Greg led the singing, his voice deep and lively. Kara noticed with growing admiration how his jocular nature and unrelenting energy sparked enthusiasm in the crowd. Obviously everyone adored him. Especially Carrie. Her eyes were never off Greg for a minute. Kara wondered if Greg was aware of Carrie's unflagging devotion. He treated her with the casual, unconscious affection of a brother, but Kara suspected that Carrie yearned for much more.

Surprisingly, Carrie came close to admitting her feelings to Kara that very evening as they sat around the campfire. Between songs she leaned over and nudged Kara. "Isn't Greg the neatest guy you ever saw?" she whispered.

Kara had to agree. She felt a little uncomfortable realizing that she shared Carrie's estimation of this attractive young man she scarcely knew. But Kara's life was far too complicated at the moment to entertain any silly romantic notions. So she forced her gaze away from Greg to the remaining purple-fringed clouds pressing the skyline. Allowing her mind to wander, she imagined animals in the dark, ethereal shapes, muted herds shifting silently across the vast phantasm of the heavens.

Moments later, breaking out of her poetic reverie, she looked back at Greg. He was leading another song, something unfamiliar but vaguely appealing . . . "What a friend we have in Jesus, all our sins and griefs to bear."

Was it possible? Kara wondered. Jesus, a friend . . . bearing one's griefs? It sounded nice, an intriguing idea. But, of course, she argued, the whole premise was irrational, preposterous. Still, Kara felt a bit perplexed. Like Ben Strickland, she had always considered religion something of a guilt trip or a soporific for the unenlightened masses. But these people sang about Jesus as if He were their most intimate friend. Could they all be crazy or deluded? Even Greg? Could this Jesus they praised, if He existed, be the same heartless God who permitted such atrocities—war, famine, disease, poverty—throughout history? If so, how could the two opposing images ever be resolved into one God whom people could love and worship?

Kara nudged the questions out of her mind. They irritated and baffled her. After all, they were age-old and unanswerable puzzles, so why should she bother to wrestle with them?

After the singing (an hour of it at least!), Greg joined Kara and Carrie. The campfire had burned down to a few glowing embers, and the night air had taken on an unmistakable chill. People were packing their things and drifting off to their cars.

"You girls ready to go?" Greg questioned, pulling on his jacket. He looked at Kara. "Didn't you bring a coat—or a sweater?"

"No." She shivered involuntarily under her long-sleeve cotton blouse. "It was warm when I left home this morning."

"Here," he said, removing his jacket and slipping it around her shoulders. "You need this more than I do."

The coat felt wonderfully warm, almost comforting. Kara smiled her appreciation. She wanted to say something, but no words came. The three gathered their gear and trekked back to the car, sharing an unspoken friendship as deliciously palpable as the brisk night air.

But the feeling of companionship was shattered as Kara climbed into the backseat while Carrie slipped into the front seat beside Greg. Kara chided herself for wishing that she could sit beside Greg and that only the two of them were together in the car. Absurd as it was, Kara found herself hoping against hope that Greg would take Carrie home first. But no such luck. She recognized the landmarks. They were heading her way.

Guilt feelings surged through Kara. *Greg is Carrie's, you dope,* she argued silently. *Don't let him invade your thoughts like this or—God forbid—your heart!*

"Did you have a good time?" Carrie asked, turning in her seat to look back at Kara.

"Yes," she replied sincerely. "It was a wonderful day."

"Then you'll have to join us again," said Greg. "The youth group has something going nearly every week."

"I really couldn't intrude—"

"Intrude?" gasped Carrie. "Oh, Kara, don't you understand? We'd love to have you with us as often as possible."

Kara laughed faintly, groping for words. "Well, you know the saying . . . three's a crowd."

"Not in this case," said Greg. "Carrie and I go back a long ways. We're good buddies, aren't we, kid?"

Carrie nodded. "Our folks have been good friends since college."

"Don't tell anyone or it would spoil my image," said Greg teasingly, "but I used to baby-sit for the squirt here."

Carrie playfully tweaked Greg's ear. "I'm not the squirt anymore, buster. I packed that name away with my dolls and coloring books."

"You're right. I stand corrected," he acknowledged. Then he stifled a chuckle.

"Okay, what's so funny?" challenged Carrie.

"Oh, nothing much," mused Greg. "I was just remembering the time when I was fourteen and you were about six and you talked me into baking cookies."

"I helped too," said Carrie with mock smugness.

"You sure did. Our folks called the fire department. They thought we were burning down the house."

"We just wanted to be sure the cookies were done," Carrie explained with a mischievous grin at Kara.

"Charcoal black is what they were," said Greg wryly. "I didn't think your folks would ever ask me to sit for you again."

"You had to promise not to exercise your culinary skills," recalled Carrie. "And I had to subsist on peanut butter sandwiches whenever you were my sitter. How I hated peanut butter!"

Greg laughed. "Don't forget, the cookies were your idea in the first place."

Carrie glanced again at Kara. "Listen to him, will you! I figured a guy his age knew how to cook. Don't you think that was a reasonable assumption, Kara?"

"I suppose so," she replied uncertainly.

"I hope your cooking skills have improved since then," Carrie told Greg in a half-serious tone.

"You'll never know," he returned smugly. He glanced back at Kara. "You see, we need a third party around just to act as referee."

"Leave me out of it, please," Kara said uneasily. "I'm strictly neutral."

"You mean I can't count on you in my camp?" queried Greg. "Why, I thought I'd won a friend tonight."

"You have," replied Kara. "Both of you have. I can't tell you how much today has meant to me." She wanted to say more, much more, but a sudden sense of self-consciousness overcame her. She could have added that her dreams tonight would be filled with lovely visions of hot dogs and swings, of bronze sunsets and campfire hymns, and of the warm, deep, spontaneous laughter of one young man—Greg Arlen.

14

*O*ver the next few weeks Kara was drawn increasingly to her two new friends, Carrie and Greg. They established a pleasant routine. Whenever Kara had Sundays off, Greg picked up the girls for church, and afterward the threesome joined a few others from the young people's class for dinner at a nearby restaurant. The group always talked energetically about their summer work, their goals, their plans for college in the fall, about who was dating whom, and what, if anything, ought to be done to improve the unity and outreach of the class. Kara usually listened silently but attentively, feeling not quite a member of the group, but not an outsider either.

She especially enjoyed listening to Greg give his little pep talks. "Pastor John says we've doubled our class size in just one year," he would say in his rich, booming voice. "That proves we must be doing something right!" And everyone would laugh in pleased agreement.

Kara thrived on her Sunday outings and found herself anticipating them days in advance. Was it because she enjoyed the amiable companionship of others her age? Yes, partly. Or because she had begun to think of Carrie as her very own sister, with genuine, surprisingly deep fondness? Yes, that too. But her ultimate motive, if she dared to admit it, was to be with Greg—to see him, hear his voice, experience those fleeting, accidental moments of closeness . . . when their hands touched in reaching for a hymnbook, when they were pushed together in a crowd, or when he leaned over to whisper a word of explanation about the sermon or some procedure of the service. He was so intent that she understand what was happening and why, and that she not misinterpret something that was said. She sensed already how much he wanted her to believe as he did. "Christ is the most important person in my life," he told her often, solemnly. The words always gave Kara a chill.

She wondered, did Greg also suspect that she was more painfully, joyously aware of his presence than of anything happening around her? An even more disturbing question: Had Carrie guessed Kara's growing affection for Greg?

Kara didn't think so. Carrie seemed as bright and happy as ever. She showed no signs of minding that the three of them spent so much time together. In fact, if the idea didn't strike Kara as a bit saccharine, she would say that the three of them delighted in one another's company.

But one Sunday afternoon in mid-August, as the three sat in a cozy restaurant eating steak sandwiches, Carrie asked Kara an unsettling question. "So how is your mother doing?" she said as if Anna were an everyday topic.

The question took Kara by surprise, snatching her breath momentarily. She purposely never mentioned her mother, except that first time when she had related briefly the incident of the fire. "She's doing all right, I guess," Kara replied evasively.

"But you said once she was in the hospital . . . badly burned," remarked Carrie. "Is she still there?"

"Yes. She will be for a long time."

"But you never talk about her."

"I try not to think of her . . . of what happened," admitted Kara.

"Is she worse?" asked Greg.

"No, I don't think so. But the doctors say her recovery will be slow and difficult."

"Don't you see her?" Greg continued, his expression showing concern.

"No, I don't," confessed Kara, her tone on the edge of defensiveness. "I don't think it would do either of us any good. Besides, Westchester is a long drive and I dread that bumpy bus ride."

"Greg and I could take you some weekend," offered Carrie with a spontaneous lilt in her voice. She looked at Greg. "Couldn't we—some Saturday? It would be fun to make the drive together."

"Sure, I don't see why not," replied Greg. "How about this coming Saturday?"

Carrie frowned. "Oh, I can't make it. Our family is going to the lake."

"I don't want to go anyway," interjected Kara. She caught herself and added, "I mean, it's not a very pleasant experience, seeing my mother the way she is now."

"But don't you understand?" prompted Carrie. "With us along it'll be easier. You won't be alone."

"No. I can't," Kara persisted. "Besides, I usually work on Saturdays."

"Are you working this coming Saturday?" asked Greg.

"Well, no, but—"

"Then it's settled," he said. "I'll drive you to Westchester on Saturday."

Kara looked at him in astonishment. "You mean, go without Carrie?"

"Sure, go ahead. I don't mind," Carrie said with a quick, wistful glance at Greg. "You'll find that Greg's always great company." She paused, then said more brightly, "And I'll feel better knowing you've seen your mother."

Kara looked questioningly at Greg.

"I'm game if you are," he said with a smile.

———

They left early Saturday morning and stopped at a pancake house for breakfast. Kara couldn't believe her incredible good fortune—an entire day with Greg to herself. Carrie, in her generous innocence, hadn't even protested at the prospect of the two of them together. Kara felt a pinch of guilt, but not enough to diminish the pleasure of being with Greg.

They arrived at the hospital around noon and went directly to Dr. Lasky's office. He greeted Kara warmly, exclaiming over how well she looked, and then heartily shook Greg's hand. "I hope you're keeping an eye on this independent young lady," he told Greg merrily.

"Not a bad idea," Greg returned with a grin.

They sat down and Kara's expression sobered as she asked, "How is Anna?"

"She's coming along. Have you seen her yet?"

"No. I thought I should come here first. The last time I saw her was rather upsetting for everyone."

The doctor sat back in his chair, his brow furrowed in contemplation. "The question you asked me that day—I suppose you've learned the truth by now—?"

Kara glanced uneasily at Greg. "Yes, I have, but I don't want to talk about it now."

"I understand. I figured that's why you haven't been back all these weeks to see Anna."

"I suppose that's part of it. Has—has Anna asked for me?"

"She says very little. She's still withdrawn and very despondent. She may be blocking out the past."

"Have you begun the skin-grafting yet?"

"Yes, several weeks ago. She came through her first operation quite well. Another is scheduled for next week."

"How many more operations will she need?"

"We can't say for sure," replied Dr. Lasky, shifting in his chair. "It depends on how well the grafts take." He stood up then and ambled to the door. "Come. We'll talk some more on the way to the burn unit. Then I have patients I must see before lunch. You're welcome to join me in the hospital cafeteria later for a bite to eat, although I honestly can't recommend the food."

"Thanks anyway," said Kara, "but we had a huge breakfast, and I couldn't eat a thing now. I just want to see Anna." *And get it over with,* she could have added, but didn't. As they followed Dr. Lasky down the hall, Kara told him, "I really appreciate your time and concern. I feel like Anna isn't quite so alone with you here."

"Well, I always have time for you and your mother, Kara, my girl, but I can't take your place with Anna. She needs you." The doctor paused before a door that read, BAROMEDICAL UNIT. He nodded toward the window below the sign. "You want to know about your mother's treatment? Well, we've used the hyperbaric chamber with some success. The oxygen brings faster healing to Anna's body."

Kara stared through the window at two long glass cylinders with narrow beds attached on metal roller-bars. On the side of each chamber was a long panel containing numerous buttons and dials. Kara shook her head somberly. "They look like glass tombs," she murmured.

"Don't they use those to treat divers with the bends?" questioned Greg.

Dr. Lasky nodded. "Yes, but we also use this treatment now for a variety of diseases."

"But Anna still needs the skin grafting?" questioned Kara.

"That's right. The grafting is absolutely necessary." Dr. Lasky looked at Kara with a troubled earnestness. "Perhaps you can encourage Anna. I'm afraid she expected the operation to return her skin magically to normal. She has to realize it will never be that."

"How bad will it be?"

Reluctantly Dr. Lasky replied, "My dear, Anna will sustain a certain amount of deformity for the rest of her life."

Kara flinched involuntarily. She had known this all

along, but the idea put into words brought the truth home sharply. Tears stung her eyes. "How—how can I possibly help Anna? What can I say?"

"Right now she needs to be reassured about the donor sites—the undamaged areas of her body that we need for grafts. I've tried to talk to her several times about it, but she still feels we are needlessly scarring her further."

"I can understand her feelings about that," replied Kara, gazing down at her own still faintly scarred hands and arms. "That feeling of being damaged, it—it never goes away."

In an unexpected gesture of compassion, Greg put his arm around Kara and squeezed her shoulder gently. "Do you want me to go in with you to see your mother?" he asked softly.

She shook her head. "I'd better go in alone." She put on the sterile cap and gown that Dr. Lasky handed her, and with more bravery than she felt, pushed open the double doors to the burn unit. The smells, the sights, the revolting familiarity of pain and death struck Kara afresh just as she knew they would.

Seeing Anna again was even worse—the bandages, the frail, listless body, the pain-filled face with still barely recognizable features, pitiable and repellant at the same time. Kara reflected darkly, *If the sight and smell of Anna turns my stomach, how must she feel about herself!*

Gingerly she approached the bed and said with forced brightness, "Hello, Anna."

Anna looked at her with blank, exhausted eyes.

"Anna, it's me, Kara. How are you feeling today?"

Slowly the woman's dark-rimmed eyes grew intent with recognition. In a low, accusing voice she rasped, "Why didn't you let me die in the fire!"

Kara, taken aback, stammered, "I—I couldn't—!"

Anna turned her head slightly. "They are . . . killing me

here, Kara. They operated and made new scars. It didn't even
help. Look at me!"

"You're getting better, Anna. Dr. Lasky says so."

"No, I'm not. I don't want to live. There's nothing left."

"You still have me," said Kara plaintively, without conviction.

Anna searched Kara's eyes with a desperation bordering
on hysteria. "You . . . you must hate me . . . don't you hate
me? Everything that happened is my fault. Everything! I did
it. I destroyed everything!"

"No, you didn't," argued Kara, but even as she spoke,
she knew she did blame Anna for the fire.

"Tell Dr. Lasky . . . no more operations. Tell him . . . let
me go home . . . die in peace."

Kara felt an overwhelming weariness descend on her.
She was silent, knowing she couldn't tell Anna there was no
house, no place to go. How could Anna think their home had
survived? Kara couldn't cope with any of this—Anna's pre-
carious physical condition, her deep depression and seemingly hopeless future, not to mention Kara's own bitterness
and resentment. (Did Anna even suspect that Kara had
learned the truth about her heritage?)

A minute passed. And another. Compulsively Kara
pushed words through her lips—bland, hurried bits of information tidily varnished to reflect better circumstances than
she possessed. She raved on foolishly about her well-paying
job, her lovely apartment, her many attentive friends. She
purposely neglected mentioning Carrie Seyers, for the Seyers
name would likely rouse suspicion. Kara was not ready to
confront Anna with the brutal fact that she knew she was not
Ben and Anna's daughter. Knowing that might kill Anna.

After what seemed an interminable period of time, a
nurse approached Anna's bed with a tray and a paper cup of
pills. Kara sighed with relief. Here was her chance to make a

polite exit. Stepping away from the bed, she gave the nurse an appreciative smile.

The woman nodded her greetings and proceeded to pour Anna a glass of water. Holding it to Anna's lips, she said pleasantly, "Here's your pain medication, Mrs. Strickland. You rest now and I'll be back shortly to change your dressings." She smiled approvingly as Anna swallowed the pills, then continued in her smooth, efficient voice. "Yesterday you had a little trouble raising your arms, but maybe today you'll feel stronger."

While the nurse wrote something on Anna's chart, Kara said a brief goodbye, promising to return very soon—a week, ten days. Then she left the burn unit with the urgency of a convict escaping his cell, and nearly collapsed against Greg who was waiting for her in the hall. He helped her to the car, watching her with obvious concern. "Are you going to be all right?" he asked before starting the engine.

"Yes, I'm fine," she said contritely. "I feel so foolish . . . but for a moment there I thought I might faint."

Greg gave her an uneasy smile. "I thought so too."

"I didn't expect it to be so hard, seeing my mother again," she said.

"How is she?" queried Greg as he pulled out into the late afternoon traffic.

"She's doing as well as can be expected," replied Kara. She smiled grimly. "I guess that sounds like the doctors' stock answer."

"Sometimes that's all you can say. Now let me ask . . . how are you?"

Kara shrugged. "I really don't know. When I see Anna like that—a stranger really, nothing like the Anna I've always known—I feel so many conflicting emotions. Hopelessness . . . pity . . . guilt. I want to run away, forget what happened." Kara paused and breathed deeply, closing her eyes. "Oh, Greg," she said with a tone of self-loathing, "in a way, right now, I think I just want Anna dead."

"You're brave to admit that," observed Greg.

"Brave? You must be kidding!"

"No. Most people would try to sugarcoat their feelings, but you seem willing to face yours head on, honestly, whether good or bad. I like that about you."

"I'll take that as sort of a left-handed compliment," mused Kara. "Thank you."

"But I must confess something else," Greg went on.

"What?"

"Our trip today has raised more questions in my mind about you than it has answered."

"That sounds rather ominous."

"No, just intriguing. You make me want to know more."

"I'm glad, Greg," responded Kara, "but I'm sorry too, because I can't answer any of your questions right now. Maybe someday—"

He smiled tolerantly. "It's all right, Kara. I have no right to ask you any questions anyway." He tossed her an impulsive grin. "Except one. Would you like to stop for dinner at that restaurant just up the road?"

"I'd love to," she replied with undisguised enthusiasm. But in her heart and mind she realized she was saying much more. Irresistibly, inevitably, she wanted to cry, *Greg, I love you!*

15

Over a week passed before Kara saw Greg or Carrie again. She had feigned a headache on the Sunday morning after her trip to Westchester, feeling guilty at the prospect of attending church with Greg while Carrie was out at the lake. Her Saturday with Greg had been more than she dared hope for, but it would be wrong to push her luck, to risk betraying Carrie, her own sister. In spite of her growing feelings for Greg, Kara would have to remember that Carrie had first claim on his affections.

After church the following Sunday, Greg dropped the two girls off at Carrie's house, where Kara was staying for dinner. She had been a guest in the Seyers home several times since that first uneasy visit, and with relief Kara had noted a mellowing in her father, Wilson Seyers. He had no longer eyed her with ominous suspicion but appeared now to regard her with a sort of grudging tolerance. Perhaps he realized at last that Kara had no desire to stir up trouble or to reveal the truth about her parentage. Perhaps in time he would even come to accept her, if not as a daughter, as a friend.

After dinner Kara and Carrie took a walk to enjoy the early September sunset. Carrie was eager to hear about Kara's trip to Westchester and how Anna was faring. Kara filled her in, but minimized any reference to Greg. "Anna underwent her second skin-grafting operation on Friday," related Kara. "I telephoned Dr. Lasky yesterday and he told me she's doing just fine."

"You didn't go back for the surgery?"

"No. I had to work. I'll try to go see her next weekend."

"Maybe Greg and I can take you."

"Yes, maybe," nodded Kara.

"Didn't it help to have Greg go with you last time?"

"Oh, yes. He was wonderful company."

"I told you," Carrie smiled. "There's nobody like him." Her voice took on a pleased confidentiality as she continued, "I think I'm making progress, Kara. Have you noticed how attentive Greg has been to us lately?"

"What do you mean?"

"I mean the way he drives us to church so often and sits with us when we go out for dinner with the group."

"Hasn't he always driven you to church?" asked Kara, surprised.

"No, he had no reason to before. I rode with my folks. But since we started driving you, it's given us a reason to be together. I guess I should thank you, Kara."

"No, please don't. I'm the one who should say thanks. You two have become my . . . my best friends."

Carrie smiled widely. "I feel that way about you too, Kara. There's a special closeness between us. And that's why I want to tell you something I've never told anyone else."

Kara stared at Carrie with a mixture of curiosity and foreboding. "Are you sure you should?"

"Yes. I've been dying to tell someone. I believe . . . I feel God has shown me . . . Kara, someday, I'm going to be Greg's wife!"

"Greg's . . . wife?"

"Yes. We've been friends for years. But someday he's going to realize that we belong together. Wouldn't that be wonderful?"

Kara looked away quickly. She wasn't sure what her expression might reveal. "I hope for whatever makes you happy," she mumbled vaguely. Knots of guilt and pain constricted her throat muscles. "Maybe we should head back to the house now," she suggested.

Carrie nodded. In silence they turned around and began to retrace their steps. Finally Carrie looked earnestly at Kara and asked, "What do you plan to do?"

Startled, Kara searched Carrie's eyes. "Do about what?"

"About your future. Sometimes I feel that you're letting yourself just drift along, without purpose."

Kara shrugged. "I guess my goal is just to survive from one day to the next."

"But that's not enough," protested Carrie. "I think you need to decide what you want to do with your life. Have you ever asked yourself where you want to be by this time next year?"

Kara gave Carrie a mildly exasperated glance. "Next year? I don't even know where I want to be next week."

"Well, I've been thinking about it," said Carrie, "and I think you should enroll at City College."

"College?"

"Yes. You'll be getting the money from your father's estate soon, won't you?"

"Yes. The lawyer said the first check should arrive next week."

"Okay, so you can quit your job at Hamburger Hamlet and go to school full time. You could even take one of Greg's literature courses."

Kara slowed her pace, her mind contemplative. "Before my father died, I was going to attend the state university. I thought about becoming a doctor, like him."

"A doctor, really? That's what I call an ambitious goal."

"No," said Kara soberly. "It was a fantasy wish. I wanted to be a replica, a carbon copy of my father. I thought that would please him, even though, to tell you the truth, I hated science. But now Ben Strickland is gone, and so is any desire to be a doctor."

"I'm sorry," said Carrie as they walked up the steps of the Seyers home. "It must be awful losing your father. I can't imagine it."

Kara shrugged off Carrie's sympathy and deliberately changed the subject. "I have to admit you're right about setting goals," she reflected. "I need to do that." Then, as Carrie opened the front door, Kara said resolutely, "I think I'll do it. I'll enroll at City College next week. It has to be better than the Hamburger Hamlet!"

Carrie laughed and gave her an impulsive hug. "That's wonderful, Kara! And just think! A year from now I'll be in college too!"

———

College was a brand-new world for Kara, vastly more complex and unpredictable than high school had been. The first week of orientation was a dizzying whirlwind of activity. There were class cards to fill out, schedules to arrange, advisors to consult, books to buy, and classrooms to locate on the sprawling, urban campus.

During orientation week, Kara worked the evening shift at the Hamburger Hamlet, but on the Friday before classes began, she quit her job. That same evening she moved into an efficiency apartment near the campus. Greg and Carrie helped her move her few belongings, and afterward they went out for pizza to celebrate Kara's new home (minus roaches!) and the new school year.

With the monthly checks from her father's estate, Kara figured she would have enough to live on and maybe even a little extra for some attractive clothes. The fire had taken her entire wardrobe, but most of her outfits had been rather plain and outdated anyway. Now she wanted garments with some flair and color. She wanted to look her best—not only for Greg, but also for herself. So on Saturday she went shopping and bought two new outfits and some makeup, and even dared to have her long auburn-brown hair styled flatteringly in a shorter, more sophisticated look.

Greg noticed the difference in her appearance the moment she climbed into his car on Sunday morning. "You sure do look nice," he told her approvingly. Several times during the service she felt his eyes on her in quiet, unobtrusive admiration. She felt good, deliciously warm inside, knowing he liked the way she looked.

Greg was ready with another compliment when Kara entered his classroom early Monday afternoon. "College life must agree with you," he told her on the sly, winking.

She laughed impulsively. "I don't know. This is only my first day."

"When's your last class?"

"Three."

"How about meeting me afterward at the little restaurant around the corner?"

Kara glanced around, flustered, as other students filtered in and sat down. "I don't know if I should," she mumbled. The buzzer sounded then, so Kara nodded her assent and promptly took the nearest seat. She felt embarrassed and self-conscious. She didn't want the rest of the class to think Mr. Arlen was playing favorites.

Two hours later, as Kara and Greg sat together in a corner booth, sipping coffee and enjoying some warm apple fritters, she still felt a bit awkward. "What if your other students see us together?" she asked cautiously.

Greg chuckled. "So what? I'm on my own time now. Besides, if you want the truth, that's why I didn't suggest the campus snack shop."

Kara laughed in spite of herself. "So you *are* concerned about appearances."

"Let's just say I don't want you stuck with the label, 'Teacher's pet.'"

Kara considered telling Greg it wouldn't matter at all,

but then she thought better of the idea. Instead she said, "I enjoyed your literature class today."

"Thanks," he replied, smiling. "I think we'll be reading some stories and plays you'll like. Some fine women writers too—Flannery O'Connor, Katherine Mansfield, Tillie Olsen, Shirley Jackson—"

"Oh, yes, I remember Shirley Jackson. She wrote 'The Lottery.' I read it in high school. It was creepy."

"It's also a masterpiece of short-story writing," said Greg, draining his coffee cup. "But I'll save my speech for the classroom, okay?"

"Okay, but I don't mind listening. I want to learn all I can."

"With that attitude you'll do fine. I hope you're pleased with your first day of classes."

"I am. Art appreciation looks like fun, and so does psychology. But I'm not looking forward to history or biology. I hate memorizing dates and cutting up bugs."

"Me too," said Greg. He glanced at his watch. "Say, I've got to run, but we'll do this again real soon, all right?"

"I'd love to," replied Kara. She thought unintentionally of Carrie, who would also have loved to have been here with Greg right now. Nudging the thought away, she reasoned silently, *I'm no competition for Carrie anyway, not if God really has promised that she'll be his wife.*

"Ready to go?" said Greg, standing up and putting some change on the table.

Kara stood up too. "Yes, I am. Thanks for the coffee and conversation."

"Until next time," he said pleasantly, his gaze lingering until she turned away.

———

In the weeks that followed, Kara and Greg made several more visits to the little restaurant. There, in their corner booth, they shared convivial hours of chitchat over a milk-shake or a hamburger, and carried on absorbing discussions about the stories of Chekhov, Hemingway, and Kafka, or dissected the autobiographical elements in Tennessee Williams's poignant drama *The Glass Menagerie.*

Kara treasured these moments of intense, stimulating conversation with Greg. Never before had anyone opened her eyes to the lovely nuances and the variegated hues of good literature. Greg made the authors and their works come alive for her. Occasionally she wondered, Was it because he was such an excellent, insightful teacher?—or because Kara was in love with the instructor? Undoubtedly, both were true.

Around the middle of October Kara took time out from her studies to make two visits to Westchester to see Anna. Both times Greg and Carrie accompanied her. Although Anna was improving physically, her mental attitude remained poor. After each visit Kara found herself drained, her spirits plunging precariously. It took her days to get her emotions back on track. How glad she was that she had her classes to occupy her time and thoughts.

But late one afternoon Kara's thoughts were diverted abruptly from both Anna and her studies. She was leaving the campus after her last class when she spotted a man talking confidentially with a small group of students. Even before she realized who he was, she felt a strangely familiar abhorrence. With full recognition came a sudden sickening sensation. It was Al Price—the same swaggering stance, the sneering lips, the open shirt, the flashing medallion on his chest.

Kara stopped and considered turning back, going the other way. But too late. Al spotted her. A slow, sly smile drew his lips into a malicious arc. He excused himself from his little entourage of attentive listeners and approached Kara with a confident gait.

Kara started to walk away quickly, pretending in vain that she hadn't recognized Al. But he caught up with her and clasped her arm menacingly. "Where to, little lady?" he said.

"None of your business," she replied in a crisp, formal voice. She hoped desperately that he would get the hint and leave her alone. Or perhaps some student or professor would notice that he was a stranger, that he didn't belong on campus, that he was harassing the students. One student. Kara. But no one paid him the slightest bit of attention.

"My car is right here," he said gruffly, his face too close to hers, his hand still gripping her arm. "Can I drop you somewhere?"

"No, I can walk," she replied sharply, struggling to pull away.

"You've said no once too often," he hissed, and brusquely steered her toward the automobile. He pushed her inside, then climbed behind the wheel and sped off before Kara could think or react. She sat stiffly, while a chilling terror swept over her. This couldn't be happening. Surely Al couldn't be so brazen as to kidnap her in broad daylight from a busy campus. But he had told her once that she would be sorry for the way she had treated him. Was this what he meant? In what unspeakable way would he get his revenge?

"Where are you taking me?" she managed to whisper.

"To your apartment. Same place, isn't it?"

"No," she said quickly. "I—I moved."

He glanced suspiciously at her. "You kidding me?"

"No, I did move. Honest. I hated that other place."

"So where are you now?"

Kara's thoughts raced. If Al learned where she was living now, he might never leave her alone. She would never feel safe.

"I—I'm not going home," she blurted.

"Then where are you going?"

"To a friend's house," she rushed on nervously. "For dinner. She's expecting me right now."

Grudgingly, Al said, "Okay, so where does your friend live?"

"Uh—it's the Wilson Seyers home on Acacia. He's the editor of the city paper, you know. A very important man in town."

Al scowled at her. "So you know the Seyers family, huh? Well, whaddaya know." He sat forward slightly and accelerated the engine, propelling the car well past the speed limit. He was silent for the rest of the drive.

Minutes later he pulled up with a screech in front of the Seyers home. "Get out, duchess," he snarled, reaching across to push open her door. "You win this time."

She scurried out of the car only moments before he raced the motor and peeled off down the street. She stood staring after him, perplexed, unnerved, but immensely relieved to be rid of Al Price so easily. Now she would have to figure out a way to explain her unexpected visit to the Seyers home at dinnertime.

16

"Surprise," said Kara in a small, apologetic voice when Carrie opened her front door.

Carrie's expression flashed from perplexity to pleasure. "Why, Kara, what are you doing here?"

"Please don't ask," said Kara. "I—I couldn't explain if I tried."

"Well, come in. We're just sitting down to dinner. Won't you join us?"

"Oh, no, I don't want to intrude—"

"But you're not. Mother will be glad to set an extra plate."

Kara followed Carrie inside and politely greeted Mr. and Mrs. Seyers, already seated at the table. Lynn Seyers stood up and promptly set another place beside Carrie while Wilson eyed Kara with mild curiosity. "I didn't know you girls were planning to spend the evening together," he mused.

"It was sort of a last-minute thing," offered Carrie obliquely.

Kara sat down, feeling foolish. She shouldn't have insisted that Al Price bring her here. But she had felt so terrified. What else could she have done? Then, as she glanced around the table, she realized there was a tension in the room that had nothing to do with her presence.

"Where's Danny?" she asked, making conversation.

"That's what I want to know," replied Wilson, his voice edged with irritation.

"He hasn't come home from school yet," admitted Lynn.

"But that was hours ago!" snapped Wilson. "Where is he!"

"I don't know."

"This has happened too many times lately," continued Seyers. "That boy has got to learn some responsibility around here. He can't just come and go as he pleases."

"Even when he does come home, he goes directly to his room and won't speak to anyone," remarked Carrie. "He's sure no fun to be around anymore."

"His grades are slipping too," said Lynn with concern. "I wish I knew what to do. I guess we just have to trust the Lord for him."

Wilson cleared his throat deliberately. "I hardly think this is something we should discuss before company," he said, giving Kara a small, detached smile.

"It's all right, really," said Kara. "I care about Danny too."

"Well, that's kind of you," said Lynn, placing her napkin in her lap, "but I hope Danny is just going through one of those teenage phases most kids go through."

"I suggest we eat before the food gets cold," interjected Wilson sharply.

Carrie prayed briefly for God's blessing on the food and for His protection over Danny. As everyone ate in silence, Kara chided herself for intruding on the privacy of the Seyers family. This definitely wasn't the way to win friends—or new-found fathers.

Halfway through the meal Danny burst in the door, flung his coat and books on a chair, and approached the dinner table with a scowl. "You guys eating already?" he muttered.

"This is our usual time, in case you've forgotten," said Wilson severely. "Now go wash your hands, young man, and then sit down."

"All right already," snapped the boy. "Just keep your shirt on!"

While Danny trudged to the kitchen, Lynn put her hand on her husband's arm to restrain him, and whispered, "Please, Will, let's have a peaceful dinner."

"Peaceful?" seethed Wilson, his face red with rage. "How can we have a peaceful meal when that boy is so blatantly disrespectful?"

Danny returned to the table, took his seat, and sullenly helped himself to the food.

"So where were you?" demanded his father.

"At a friend's," replied Danny without looking up.

"What friend?"

"Nobody you know."

"Try me."

"Just a kid at school. Pete somebody."

"You mean you don't even know his last name?"

"What's it to you, Dad?" challenged Danny, spooning gravy onto his mashed potatoes.

"It matters plenty to me," Wilson answered, his nostrils flaring slightly. "I don't like the way you've been behaving lately, and I don't think much of your attitude either." He paused and gave Kara a sidelong glance. "And it makes me furious that we should have to get into this when we have a guest in the house."

"Aw, you always gotta have something to crab about," complained Danny, his eyes hard and reproachful.

Wilson rose halfway out of his seat. "You haven't heard anything yet, young man!"

"Well, if it's true confessions you want," retorted the boy, "I could say plenty about you!"

"Wilson, Danny, please! Let's eat now and talk later," urged Lynn.

Wilson looked from Danny to his wife to Kara. "Yes, all right," he said with a disgruntled sigh.

Everyone continued to eat, stiffly, politely, enduring the electric tension in the room. After a few minutes, Lynn asked with forced cheerfulness, "How was your day at the office, dear?"

"Same as usual," Wilson grunted.

"Surely some interesting things must be happening?"

Wilson looked up, perturbed, and blotted his lips with his napkin. "What do you want to hear, Lynn?"

"I don't know. I just thought—"

"So you want the latest religious editorial?"

A grimace of pain crossed Lynn's face. "Will, please—"

His shoulders sagged slightly. "I'm sorry for the sarcasm, Lynn. To answer your question more fairly, there is the new series of articles I'm running. I mentioned them before. Wrote them myself, in fact. The first is in today's paper."

"Oh, I haven't seen the paper yet," said Lynn.

"What's the series about, Dad?" asked Carrie.

"Teenage drug pushers."

"Hasn't that subject been covered in the past?" queried Lynn.

"Yes, and I suppose some people no longer consider it a serious problem. They figure everything has been said, so let's go on to something else. But I don't feel that way."

"Why not, Will?"

"Because drugs are a continuing problem in our high schools, and in our junior high schools too. In many instances, it's even reaching down to the grade schools."

"What a tragedy," said Lynn, shaking her head. "To think of children taking drugs."

"And it's not just pot anymore," remarked Carrie. "Crack is a cheap form of cocaine that's pretty easy for kids to get—and it's so dangerous that some kids have died the first time they've tried it! I've also heard that PCP—'Angel Dust'—is really popular. That stuff can scramble your brains for good."

Wilson nodded grimly. "It'll fill our cemeteries and mental institutions if we don't stop it. Did you know the average age of users used to be nineteen? Now it's fourteen."

"How is PCP used?" asked Lynn.

"Sometimes in liquid form, sprayed on mint leaves or even on a marijuana joint," replied Wilson. "But some kids sniff PCP powder. That's where the name 'Angel Dust' comes from."

"What an ironic name for something straight out of hell," observed Carrie soberly.

"More mashed potatoes, please," interrupted Danny. He nudged Carrie impatiently. "I said, potatoes, please."

Carrie handed the bowl to him but kept her eyes on her father. "Tell us more about your series of articles, Dad."

"I'm running them on the front page," he told her, his pale gray eyes narrowing. "But I'm just sorry the point of today's article has to be brought home so dramatically."

"What do you mean?" asked Lynn.

Wilson's expression was grave as he replied, "A seventh grader at Montgomery Junior High died yesterday of a drug overdose. His friends claim he got the stuff from a high schooler."

"Who died?" asked Danny suddenly.

"A boy named Jeremy Helms," said Wilson.

Danny's fork clattered against his plate.

"What's the matter, Danny?" questioned his father. "Did you know the boy?"

"No, never heard of him," returned Danny with an edge of defensiveness. He pushed back his chair and stood up abruptly. "I have homework to do," he announced, his voice raw, uneven. He escaped to his room before anyone could manage a reply.

17

One evening nearly a week after Kara's unplanned visit to the Seyers home, she received a puzzling phone call from Carrie. Carrie's voice sounded muffled and strained, and (was Kara imagining it?) she seemed disturbingly on the verge of losing control. "Kara, can you come over right away?" Carrie urged. "It's important."

"I suppose I can," Kara replied uncertainly. "But I'll have to take a cab."

"Please come right away. We need to talk."

"What's wrong?" questioned Kara. "Can you give me some idea?"

"No. Just come. Goodbye." With that the receiver went dead.

When Kara arrived at the Seyers home a half hour later, Carrie, her eyes damp and melancholy, ushered her inside with a quiet warning. "The folks are away for the evening, but Danny's in his room. I don't want him to hear us."

"What is it?" whispered Kara. "What happened? Is it Danny?"

"No," said Carrie as they entered her room and shut the door. The room was dark except for one dim lamp by the bed. Carrie sat down, grabbed a tissue, and blew her nose. "I—I don't want to cry—"

"You've been crying," said Kara softly.

"Yes. I didn't intend to. It—it was just such a shock."

Carrie stood up and approached Kara with guarded steps. The shadows cut harshly into her round, sensitive face. Kara couldn't read her expression, except for her eyes. They were large and luminous and unbearably sad as she said, "You didn't tell me . . . you never said a word—"

Kara felt her pulse begin to race. "What are you talking about?"

"You. You, Kara. You were my friend. I thought that was all there was to it. But you had your own reason for coming here. It's true, isn't it?"

Kara caught her breath. "What—what's true?"

Carrie looked away, biting her lip. Then her eyes riveted on Kara. Her voice broke as she asked, "Are you my sister?"

The question penetrated like a knife. Finally Kara murmured, "How did you find out?"

"Then it's so? It's not some outrageous game?"

"No, Carrie. It's true. Your father . . . is my father."

Carrie sank back on her bed and sighed audibly. "It's too incredible!"

"Who told you?"

"Danny. He says he's known for several weeks."

"But how? I haven't told anyone."

Carrie looked up searchingly. "Why didn't you tell me? We were so close. You could have told me."

"No, I couldn't. I wanted to. I hated having our friendship based on a lie. But I promised your father that I would say nothing. I had to keep my word. It was the only way he would let me be part of your lives. I didn't want to lose you all when I had just found you." Kara sat down beside Carrie and said intently, "Please tell me. How did Danny find out?"

"He overheard my parents talking," replied Carrie shakily.

"I guess Mother had suspected something for a long time. She thought you looked like Daddy and that sometimes your gestures were uncannily the same. And Daddy was always so nervous and distracted around you."

Kara's voice was thick with remorse. "I shouldn't have forced myself into your lives. It was a stupid, selfish thing to do."

"No. I'm glad now that I know," insisted Carrie.

"But Danny—this must be why he's been so troubled lately."

"That's part of it, I suppose, but I think there's more, something else, something he hasn't shared with any of us."

"How much did he hear . . . about me . . . about his father?"

Carrie stood up and brushed her fingers through her hair. "He heard it all, the whole story. At least, I assume it's the whole story. Dad told Mother about his relationship with your mother, Catherine Hardin. And he told Mom he never knew about you until the day you walked into his office—the day we met."

"What did your mother say?" ventured Kara.

"I don't know. But she's known for weeks now and hasn't treated you any differently."

"No, she hasn't," marveled Kara. "She's always warm and gracious and kind."

"It's Danny I'm worried about," said Carrie. "When he told me about you, he sounded so bitter toward our father. At first I thought he was making it up, the story sounded so preposterous. I thought he was being a brat because he was angry with Dad. But then I saw the look on his face and I knew he was telling the truth."

"Do you think I should try to talk to him?"

"No. I think we should leave him alone for a while. Like I said, he has some other things on his mind lately too. I think he needs time to work them out."

Kara stood up, walked over, and put her hand on Carrie's arm. "I'm glad you know the truth, Carrie," she said gently. "Now there are no secrets between us."

Carrie managed a smile. "No, no secrets."

"Please say you won't hate me because of what's happened."

Carrie hugged Kara briefly, impetuously. "Oh, I would never, never hate you!" she exclaimed.

"But what about your father?" persisted Kara. "Can you forgive him?"

Carrie brushed tears from her eyes. "Of course I forgive him, Kara. Christ forgave me for all my sins that took Him to the cross to die. How could I not forgive my own father?"

Kara sighed with relief. "You don't know how glad I am that there won't be hard feelings in your family because of me."

A troubled expression crossed Carrie's face. "Well, I can only speak for myself, Kara. I want us to be close. And I'd never hold a grudge against my father. He didn't even know you existed, and he owes me no explanation for his past." She hesitated, fixing her dark, worried eyes on Kara. "But I don't know about Danny. I don't know if he'll ever be able to accept the truth or forgive our father."

18

After her Friday classes, Kara met Greg for their usual rendezvous at the nearby restaurant. He was already in their favorite corner booth, sipping his coffee and scanning some papers. He grinned broadly as she sat down. "I hoped you could make it," he said, pushing the papers aside.

"Test papers?" she queried, setting her books beside her. "Yep. Thought I'd sneak in a little work until you arrived." Reading her expression, he added wryly, "I haven't come across your exam yet."

"Oh, it's just as well. I was horribly wordy," she confessed. "What do you call it—verbose? You'll probably flunk me on the spot."

"I'll try not to," he teased.

"Will we discuss the test in class next week?" asked Kara. "Essay questions are so—so complex, so variable. I'd like to hear what the others wrote."

"You will," Greg assured her. "It should make an invigorating session."

Kara smiled. "I wrote an entire page on James Joyce's short story 'The Dead.' I thought the snow was both real and a metaphor . . ."

"Very perceptive," observed Greg, watching her with quiet amusement.

"And the music, too, the repetition of music—I felt it had special significance like the snow—" She looked up at Greg, her eyes narrowing. "Are you laughing at me?"

"No, not at all. I like hearing your opinions."

"But you're the expert, not me."

"Don't belittle yourself. You have a keen sensitivity to literature. You just might discover that you're a born writer."

Kara laughed. "Oh, Greg, I wish!"

"Say, we haven't ordered you any coffee yet. I'll get a waitress—"

"No, wait. I don't want any coffee."

"Then something else—a sandwich, soft drink?"

"No," Kara replied firmly. "Greg, I have to talk to you. Could we go somewhere . . . for a drive perhaps?"

Greg's brows furrowed slightly. "Is something wrong?"

"Not exactly. There's just something you should know. I'd like to tell you in private."

"Sounds important. Let's go," he replied and promptly gathered his papers and stuffed them into his briefcase.

They drove several miles out of town through a scenic, rural area east of Claremont. The sun hovered on the skyline like a huge ripe melon as Greg pulled his automobile off onto a gravel road and stopped.

"It's beautiful out here," marveled Kara.

"Well, you've had the ten-cent tour of Claremont's farmlands," Greg quipped. He nodded toward the pasture. "I hope you don't mind a few grazing cows and sheep for company."

"They look like they'll mind their own business," she laughed, but her laughter was edged with nervousness.

Greg shifted slightly to face her. "What is it, Kara? What's the problem?"

She was silent for a minute, sorting her thoughts. Finally she said, "Greg, do you remember the first time you drove me home to Westchester? You said the trip raised more questions about me than it answered. Well, now I want to answer some of those questions."

He glanced away. "I said then and I'll say again, you don't owe me any explanations."

"But I want to," said Kara. "It's out in the open now. I don't want any more secrets."

"Secrets?"

"Yes. For months now I've felt like a—a hypocrite. I didn't plan it. Carrie and I met by accident. I couldn't tell her who I was. Then as we became friends, it seemed like such a great opportunity to get to know her family—"

"Kara, what are you trying to say?"

She paused and looked seriously at him. "I'm saying . . . Carrie is my sister. Wilson Seyers is my father."

Greg stared at her with an expression of incredulity that silenced her momentarily. "I didn't expect a revelation like this," he managed at last. "I've known the Seyers all my life, and not once did Will ever give the slightest hint that he had another child—"

"He didn't know," interrupted Kara.

"Didn't know?" Greg asked in surprise.

"Neither did I until a few months ago." She began the account then, covering the incidents as Catherine Hardin had related them to her, speaking dispassionately, as if it had all happened to someone else—some elusive, imaginary character from a story in Greg's literature course perhaps.

When she had finished, Greg emitted a long, low whistle and said, "Unbelievable. I don't know what to say."

"Don't say anything. I'm just glad you know."

"How did Will react when you first told him?"

"He didn't believe me at first. Then he was very angry that I was forcing myself into his life. Now I think he tolerates me for Carrie's sake."

"And how does Carrie feel now that she knows the truth?"

"She's been wonderful!" exclaimed Kara as she changed her position in the cramped front seat of Greg's car. "She's accepted me as her sister *and* friend."

"That's Carrie for you," grinned Greg. "She's one terrific girl."

Kara flinched slightly at Greg's sudden ebullience over Carrie, then silently scolded herself for her pettiness. "I wish I were as kind and generous as Carrie," she murmured.

"You are. You're alike in many ways."

Kara smiled grimly. "Don't I wish. Carrie was so understanding and forgiving. I was afraid she might be angry with me or her father. But she said . . ."

Greg waited. "Yes, what did she say?"

"She said she could forgive others because Christ had forgiven her."

"That's true."

"It sounds so . . . like a cliché. But the way she said it . . . like she really meant it."

"Don't you think she did?"

Kara nodded. "I think that's what she believes—"

"It's what I believe too, Kara. Don't you?"

"No, I'm afraid I'm not the religious type," she said, averting her eyes to the window to avoid Greg's gaze.

"Christ is more than a religion, Kara," said Greg gently. "He's a person. He loves you."

"Yes, I've heard all that before," she said dully. "That's what Aunt Kate says. That's what her minister and your minister say." She looked soberly at Greg. "I just don't happen to believe it."

A sadness darkened Greg's eyes as he replied, "I didn't realize that's how you felt."

"Well, the subject never came up," said Kara, gesturing nervously.

"But I thought—"

Her mouth felt unnaturally dry as she rushed on. "I might as well confess what a hypocrite I've been, Greg—going to church with you every Sunday, taking part in the youth activities, singing the hymns, when I'm not even one of you. I'm sorry."

"Perhaps one day you will believe—"

"No, I won't," Kara said firmly, wincing a little at Greg's expression of disappointment. "Don't you see? I have no intention of believing. If there's a God, He's made a mess of things—"

"No, Kara, we're the ones who make a mess of things when we choose our own way instead of God's. I know. When I was a young teenager, I rebelled against my parents' religion. But then one day I came to know Christ personally and realized He really is God."

Kara shrugged. "Well, if He is God, He could make things right. In an instant He could change the world, put the pieces back together—"

"He does, Kara. But He works quietly in individual hearts, revealing himself, healing wounds, forgiving, restoring. He chooses to change the world through people, one by one—through Carrie, Lynn Seyers, your Aunt Kate, the pastor, me—"

Kara emitted a hard, rebuking sound, not quite a laugh. "You all sound alike, Greg. I thought you of all people would be more open-minded, what with your love of literature, your insights into different viewpoints and lifestyles—"

"I *am* open-minded, Kara, where there's room for opinion. But I take a hard line on the truth."

"Yes, well, everyone has his own idea of what truth is."

"But remember, Kara, truth is no less truth just because you don't believe it."

She cleared her throat uneasily and said, "I want to go home, Greg."

Obligingly he started the engine. "Should I pick you up on Sunday morning?"

"I don't know. Now that I've told you how I feel, it would be a bit awkward—"

"I won't let it bother me."

"But it bothers me, Greg. Sometimes I feel . . . pursued . . . haunted. The words of the sermons and hymns attack me at the oddest times, when I have no reason to think of them. They stay in my mind, like irritants. It's almost like when I was a child."

"A child?"

"Yes, it's silly, but when I was little I would think of something naughty, and the harder I tried to push the thought out of my mind, the more entrenched it became. I was horrified that my parents might be able to read my mind."

"But this is different," mused Greg. "These aren't naughty thoughts."

"No, just bits and pieces of Bible verses and hymns. Do you suppose I'm being brainwashed?"

"Maybe Spirit-washed." Greg gave her a small, knowing smile. "I mean, the Holy Spirit is speaking to you, patiently coaxing you to Christ. He's your pursuer, Kara, the Ghost that haunts you. He won't relent until you surrender to Him."

"Then He has a long wait," muttered Kara. "Besides, I've had a hard enough time lately trying to figure out who I am without religion complicating things."

Greg gazed seriously at her. "Believe me, Kara, you'll never know who you really are until you see yourself through the eyes of Christ."

She looked imploringly at him. "Can't we drop this subject, Greg? I'd rather talk about . . . about James Joyce and his use of symbols."

Greg nodded, shifted his car into drive, and pulled back onto the road. Heading back toward Claremont, they made several faltering attempts at conversation and finally rode the rest of the way in silence.

Kara felt a strange relief when they entered the city limits of Claremont. But when Greg stopped for a red light at an intersection near the high school, she shuddered involuntarily.

In the lane beside them was Al Price's car! Al was looking the other way, talking to someone beside him in the front seat. Kara craned her neck cautiously to see what unsuspecting dupe would associate with Al. Her heart stopped momentarily as she recognized young Danny Seyers.

"Isn't that Danny?" she cried, gripping Greg's arm.

"What? Where?"

"In that car!" The light changed then and Al's vehicle sped away with a powerful surge, leaving Greg's car behind.

"I couldn't see," Greg admitted. "But so what if it was Danny?"

"He was with—" Kara stopped. How could she possibly explain her unpleasant association with Al Price? Greg might misinterpret things. Heaven forbid, he might even think she had led Al on. But more important now, what was Danny, a high school kid, her own half brother, doing with a shrewd, calculating operator like Al Price? Whatever the reason, if Al was involved, it spelled trouble.

19

$\mathcal{F}$or the next two weeks Kara kept her distance from everyone—Greg, the Seyers family, and the church. She figured too much had been revealed about her background and beliefs. Undoubtedly everyone knowing her true parentage, would feel uncomfortable around her now, no matter what Carrie said. Danny was hurt and angry. And surely Greg considered her a heathen. She couldn't bear to see any more pain and disappointment in their faces. So it was best to extrude herself from their lives as neatly and quietly as possible.

To prove her new independence, Kara went out and purchased a secondhand car—a green two-door Ford, six years old and just adequate. But at least now she could go where she pleased without having to depend on the bus or someone else.

Then, just when Kara thought the course of her life was fairly settled, she received a phone call from Lynn Seyers, asking her to come over that evening for a visit. Kara went reluctantly, her stomach in knots, not knowing what to expect.

Lynn greeted her graciously, and invited Kara to join her for tea and German chocolate cake at the kitchen table. No one else was at home.

"I wanted us to have a chance to talk alone," Lynn told her as she poured the tea. "I'm sorry we haven't talked sooner. You must think we've been ignoring you."

"No, not at all," said Kara. She didn't add that she purposely been avoiding *them*.

Lynn's slender fingers lightly touched the delicate china cup as she gazed at Kara, her deep, green eyes sympathetic. "Carrie told us of your last visit, so we can be honest with each other, Kara. I know who you are. I know you're Wilson's daughter." Her generous chin quivered slightly. "I know how awkward this is for you, for both of us. But I think in time we'll all adjust."

Defensively Kara said, "When I first came here, Mrs. Seyers, I never intended to cause any trouble."

"I know, dear."

"I'm not so sure your husband believes me."

"He will. You must give him time."

"I just wanted—" Kara felt her voice quaver. "I wanted to know who I really am. I wanted to know my birth father."

"I understand that, Kara. It's just that your way of getting acquainted—your approach—created some hard feelings in Will. But I truly believe things will work out."

"You mean you think someday we can all be friends?"

"I hope so. I know Carrie wants that."

"And—you?"

"I—want whatever is best for my family and whatever the Lord wants for us."

"What about Danny and my fa—I mean, Wilson?"

"That's all right, Kara. You can say it. He *is* your father. But I'm not sure what he and Danny want." Her forehead creased slightly. "Danny is young and confused right now. In fact, lately he's alienated himself from the entire family."

"Because of me?"

"I don't know, Kara. I suppose that's part of it, but I think there's more to it. Danny refuses to confide in us anymore. He's become terribly private and withdrawn."

"I'm sorry. I wish I could help him." Kara sipped her tea, then looked up earnestly at Lynn. "Do you have any idea how my father feels about me?"

"I really can't speak for him, dear. You'll have to ask him yourself when he gets home."

"You mean . . . tonight?"

"I think it would be a good idea to get things out in the open between you. It'll be healthier for all of us. Then perhaps we can begin to build a genuine friendship."

Kara shook her head. "Mrs. Seyers," she said quietly, "I thought you, of all people, would hate me."

"No, Kara. Naturally it was a shock at first, finding out who you really are and learning of Will's relationship with your mother. I admit there were tears and I spent many hours in prayer before our meeting today. But I realize now that all of these things happened before Will and I met, so I can't say he was unfaithful to me. And, of course, he didn't even know about you. So I hold no animosity toward you or Will. I want to accept you as my husband's child."

Kara blinked back tears. "I wish Wilson felt that way too."

Lynn nodded gravely. "I wish I could say he did. But you see, Kara, he and Danny don't have the Lord in their lives to help them face their problems. I think that's why things hit them harder. They see only the problems, not God's hand working through them."

Kara stared down into her tea. No sense in volunteering which side she was on in this religion issue.

Wilson arrived home shortly and, on seeing Kara, offered a tight, reserved smile. She sensed that he was surprised to see her there.

"Kara and I have had a nice talk, Will," Lynn told him as they embraced briefly. "We've cleared the air between us, and now maybe the two of you would like to do the same."

Wilson gave Kara a cryptic glance and cleared his throat nervously. "I don't know—"

"I'll straighten things here in the kitchen while you two

go in the living room," Lynn continued, ignoring his obvious indecision.

With a relenting shrug, he escorted Kara to the living room, where they sat down formally, opposite each other. For a minute they sat in silence, exchanging wary glances. Then Will said, almost gruffly, "This wasn't my idea."

"Well, it certainly wasn't mine," returned Kara curtly.

Will ran his fingers distractedly through his thinning reddish hair so that several strands remained at odd angles from his head. "Well," he said, his words clipped, "you got your own way at last, coming here and putting Lynn on the spot. I hope you're satisfied."

Kara stared at him in disbelief. "Your wife invited me. It was her idea!"

Wilson looked away, his defensive expression crumbling. "I should have known," he mumbled. "That's Lynn for you."

Kara studied him, pitying him—this strange, private man, her father. Unexpectedly she blurted, "You'll never be my father, will you!"

He stared open-mouthed at her. "What are you saying?"

"I don't know," replied Kara, baffled by her own outburst. "It's just that from the beginning I expected something, some feeling, some sort of recognition between us. I thought we'd both know instinctively that we are father and daughter, that there would be a special bond between us. But there's nothing, is there? No feelings, no responses, just this painful uneasiness, this awkwardness—"

"Perhaps someday, Kara."

She watched him curiously. Her voice took on a low, fatal tone. "How can there be . . . a tie as close as ours yet . . . there's nothing there . . . nothing at all?"

Wilson stood up and paced around his chair. "It's not that I feel *nothing*, Kara. It's just that I don't know *how* I feel. Can't you see how it is? A strange young woman walks in and says she's my daughter. I don't know you from Adam. Surely you see that. I don't know you, and you don't know me. Maybe in time feelings will come."

Kara stood up abruptly. "In time . . . in time! That's all I hear! That first day in your office, I came looking for you because I thought you could help me find out who I am. But I was wrong, terribly wrong! I'm sorry. I'm sorry for everything!" She grabbed her purse and started blindly for the door.

"Kara, wait!" Wilson approached her, his hand raised in a fleeting gesture of supplication. As soon as she stopped, he let the hand fall loosely to his side. His pale eyes were watery, nearly invisible. His ruddy complexion seemed somehow blemished. "Kara," he said, with less intensity now and a touch of frustration, "please be patient with me. It's not easy for me to change my ways. But regardless of my feelings, you are welcome in my house."

Kara stared at him, wanting desperately to shout, *Don't do me any favors!* Instead, she ran wordlessly out of the house and slammed the door, her heart pounding furiously, hot, angry tears blurring her vision.

As she drove home, she reflected darkly, with a pungent sadness, *The man who is my father will never love me like the man who was not my father.*

That evening Kara's thoughts pressed on her mind with a grim relentlessness. The strange vagaries and quirks of her life teased her mercilessly, reminding her that in pursuing her identity she had unearthed a dozen questions, paradoxes, and confusions. If anything, the essence of Kara Strickland was more elusive now than ever. She had taken an obscure pride in tracing her background, her heritage, but now she could see that her efforts were a fiasco. No one could tell her who she was, except she herself, and now suddenly she wasn't sure she wanted to know. The answer might very well be disappointing, even devastating.

After several hours of inner scrutiny, Kara recalled inadvertently what Greg had said about seeing herself through the eyes of Christ. A strange, intriguing thought, but what did it mean? Even if she could see herself through Christ's eyes, she sensed that she wouldn't measure up well there either. And yet, oddly enough, it was only the Christians she knew who seemed willing to accept her for herself, whoever she was. Carrie, Greg, Lynn Seyers, even Aunt Kate—they all showed that they cared about her.

"So where do I go from here?" she said aloud. Her voice, breaking the silence, startled her. It reminded her of how alone she was, even here in her new, clean, orderly apartment, free of insects and traffic noises. Alone. And yet she had the uneasy feeling that she was not completely alone. She sensed a presence—something—no, Someone. As incredible as it seemed, she knew who it was—the God of Greg and Carrie and Aunt Kate!

Clearly she had subjected herself to too many sermons, listened to too many Scripture verses. Irritatingly, the words stuck in her mind like glue. As irrational as it seemed, this God of theirs was here now, pursuing her when she felt most vulnerable and needy. His voice rang in her thoughts as clearly as if He spoke aloud.

Kara.

"Leave me alone," she said defiantly.

I am here, Kara.

"No. You're a figment of my imagination, an illusion, a myth!"

I am the way—

"There is no way. Or there are lots of ways. Everyone has his own way!"

—the truth—

"What is truth?"

—the life—

"No. I don't believe. I won't."

No one comes to the Father—
"I don't want to come—!"
—except by Me.

"Who are you, God? Why do you keep taunting me!" She stopped abruptly and realized she was speaking aloud to someone she had insisted did not exist. What's more, she almost expected an answer. He whom she dismissed as illusion was speaking in the silences of her mind. He whom she regarded as blind theory or madness or conjecture was confronting her with himself, urging her to face Him once and for all. His presence in the room was nearly palpable.

"Who are you?" she whispered again, a sense of awe shaping her words.

The response, *I am Jesus, whom you persecute,* came to mind, but only because Carrie's pastor had preached recently about Paul's conversion on the Damascus Road. Paul had asked the same question, *Who are you, Lord?* A universal question, reflected Kara, as perplexing and unanswerable as, *Who am I?* There was no simple, all-encompassing answer, no final authority.

Or was there? Greg and Carrie said the Bible was the ultimate authority. But wasn't Kara setting herself up as that authority by making judgments about God? Who was she to say what God was or wasn't? Who was she to pretend to know? But if she didn't know, who did? How could she trust anyone else's opinion more than she could trust her own?

The Bible. It all came back to that. She recalled that Carrie and Greg's pastor had said time and again, "Don't believe what I say because I say it. Believe it because God says it in His Word. The Bible is the final authority for truth, God's personal letter to mankind."

Kara's thoughts churned. The realization struck her that if she were genuinely interested in truth for truth's sake, she should give God a chance to prove himself to her. In the name of fairness and honest investigation.

But did she really want the truth? If God were all He claimed to be, wouldn't He have a legitimate claim on her life? Believing required commitment. Was she ready for that?

Another thought formed. If God cared about her with half as much loving concern as Carrie and Greg and Lynn Seyers showed her, she would be foolish to turn away from His love. She had to find out if such a love were possible.

Aloud she whispered, "God, if you are real, I want to believe. If you are everything the Bible says you are, I want to know and love you." She waited a minute, listening to the quiet, almost afraid to say more. In the spaces of her heart she felt a warmth, a presence, a peace.

She began to cry, the words rushing with her tears. "Oh, God, I'm sorry I doubted you. I'm sorry for all the wrong things I've done. I've been so stubborn and blind and selfish. Forgive me. Dear Jesus—" She paused, startled by the sound of His name, by her own acknowledgment of the One she had so long denied. "Dear Jesus," she repeated, her voice fragmented, emotion-filled, "please save me like you saved Greg and Carrie and Aunt Kate."

20

Kara was eager, and yet a little apprehensive, about sharing the news of her salvation with her friends. There was so much she still didn't understand and so much that she couldn't put into words. Nevertheless, she told Greg and Carrie her news just before church on Sunday morning. She had driven her own car and arrived unannounced and unexpected. When she spotted them chatting together in the vestibule, she rushed up unthinkingly and blurted, "I know Him, Carrie. He's real, just like you and Greg said!"

They both embraced her and talked at once, telling her how pleased they were. Kara listened, feeling giddy and dizzy and breathless, marveling that Greg and Carrie would treat her like a beloved family member who had come home after a very long absence.

Kara sat with Greg and Carrie in church, and during the invitation hymn she went forward, with them beside her, to make a public profession of her faith. She felt faint and tongue-tied, and her heart pulsated like a time bomb, but she was glad to be taking a stand for her new Lord. Afterward, a dozen people, including Lynn Seyers, greeted her and made her feel welcome.

After the service Kara told Carrie, "There's someone I have to talk to as soon as possible."

"Who?" asked Carrie. "My father? Your Aunt Kate?"

"No. Danny."

"Danny? I don't think you'll be able to. He won't talk to anyone anymore."

"But I have some things to say that he needs to hear from me. I think I can help him now."

"I hope you can," said Carrie. "No one else can reach him."

———————

After Kara's last class on Monday, she drove to the local high school to pick up Danny. She wasn't sure he would be there to meet her, although he had agreed halfheartedly on the phone the night before. He had refused at first to see her, but her persistence had finally persuaded him—or perhaps he had said yes just to get her off the phone.

But as Kara pulled into the high school parking lot, she noted with relief that Danny was just where he said he would be. She pulled up beside him and stopped. With a slight scowl he shuffled over to the car, opened the door, and climbed in beside her. Without a word he adjusted his books in his lap and slumped down in the seat.

"How are you today, Danny?" she asked, making conversation.

"Okay," he muttered.

She pulled out into traffic and headed for a nearby park, where she hoped they would find a private place to stop and talk. Minutes later she swung off the pavement onto a patch of gravel near a grassy slope. Here was the privacy they needed.

"So what are we doing here?" Danny asked sullenly.

"I thought we could talk without interruptions," said Kara.

"Nothing to talk about."

"I think there is." She swiveled slightly in her seat and looked closely at Danny. His freckled complexion, so much like his father's, matched his red hair. His lower lip protruded in a pout. He refused to look at her. "You're my brother, Danny," she said softly. "What do you think of that?"

"I hate it!" he snapped.

"I hated it at first too."

He gave her a curious stare. "What do you mean?"

"I mean, I was shocked and angry to learn that the people I always thought were my parents weren't. Wouldn't you be shocked too?"

He nodded grudgingly.

"Don't you think I have a right to be angry just as you are?" she asked. "I didn't choose to be your father's daughter."

"Yeah, I know. He let us all down. I wish I never had to see him again."

Kara was quiet a moment before asking, "Didn't you ever let anyone down, Danny?"

The question sparked an expression of anguish on Danny's face, but he remained stubbornly silent. Kara decided to try another tactic. "How do you know Al Price?" she asked, her voice deliberately casual.

Danny whirled around wide-eyed and demanded, "Who told you about Al Price?"

"He's sort of a friend of mine," she replied evasively.

"Al isn't anybody's friend," scoffed Danny.

"You've learned that too," Kara observed. "Then what does Al have to do with you?"

"Nothing. He just hangs around school sometimes."

"But he must have a reason—" Kara paused, recalling the day she had encountered Al on her college campus with a group of young people. Why would Al spend his time mingling with students? "Danny," she said aloud, "has Al bothered you or your friends?"

"What do you mean?"

"You know what I mean. Al Price is an immoral man. I wouldn't put anything past him."

"He's not gay, if that's what you mean," Danny retorted. "And *I'm* sure not that kind of guy."

"I didn't think so, but Al has to be up to no good. If it's not sex, I'll bet it involves money. He must be pushing something. What is it—pornography, drugs—?"

Danny winced. "I don't want to talk about Al Price."

"That's it, isn't it, Danny?"

Danny's anguished silence told her she was close to the truth. "Is it drugs, Danny? Is Al Price the one turning school kids onto drugs?"

"Naw. He's too smart for that."

"But he is involved somehow?"

"Yeah," Danny admitted slowly.

"How?" When the boy refused to answer, she demanded again, "How, Danny? Tell me!"

"Al's the source for drugs, the big man in town."

"You mean he supplies the pushers?" repeated Kara as the horror of Danny's words crept over her.

Danny nodded miserably.

"Would you be willing to go to the police and tell what you know?" she urged.

He looked at her, his eyes filled with frustration and hopelessness. "I can't." His voice was barely audible. "Because I'm one of Al's pushers."

Kara leaned back in her seat and uttered a deep sigh. "Then you must go to the police, Danny. It's the only way."

"I can't," he insisted glumly. "I—I killed someone."

"What do you mean? Who?"

"Jeremy Helms. He—he died—"

A wave of shocked disbelief swept over Kara. "You mean the seventh grader your dad talked about . . . the boy who died of a drug overdose?"

Danny pulled a handkerchief out of his pocket and blew his nose.

"You gave him the drugs?" questioned Kara.

"Yeah, I did it," Danny bawled. "I sold him the stuff. I killed him!"

Speechless, Kara put her hand on Danny's shoulder in a feeble gesture to comfort him. His body shook as he released his pent-up grief. "Are you sure?" she cried at last. "Can you be certain the drugs you sold him killed him?"

Danny awkwardly rubbed his eyes. "I sold him some of the hard stuff and three days later he was dead. He was only a seventh grader. He trusted me. I—I'm the same as a murderer."

"I know I can't begin to understand what you're going through right now, Danny," said Kara quietly, "but there is Someone who can help you and forgive you. I've just come to know Him myself."

Danny stared skeptically at her, then pulled away from her touch and looked morosely out the window. "I don't want to talk about God," he said.

"I didn't want to talk about Him either, Danny, until a few days ago when I realized God is who He says He is. It was a tremendous burden off my shoulders when I experienced Christ's love and forgiveness just by confessing my sins and asking Him into my life."

Danny shook his head defiantly. "It's too late for God— at least for me. Once you're in this racket, you can't get out from under it. They've got you tied to them for life."

"I don't believe that," said Kara. "If you go to the police, they can stop Al. They could help you get free from him."

"It wouldn't do any good," Danny whined. "Al Price covers his tracks good. Besides, it's not just Al. There are a whole bunch of guys, big shots in town, in on this thing. They're making a bundle, but the police can't get enough evidence to touch them. The only guys I can squeal on are the ones like me, guys in my class or guys in junior high. If the cops take us in, the big boys will just get themselves another bunch of flunkies to do their dirty work."

"How did you get involved in such a thing?" asked Kara soberly.

"I don't know. My buddies were doing it and they made me feel like an idiot if I didn't do it too. I didn't know how it would be. At first it was just sort of a game."

"Well, we've got to find some way to get you out of this mess," said Kara. "There has to be a way to break Al Price's cover."

"There might be a way," offered Danny, brightening slightly. "Al has this little address book. The guys talk about it, and I saw it once, just for a second. They say it contains the names of all the big shots in the drug racket here in town. They say the names are in some sort of code, but maybe if we could get ahold of that book, the police could break the code."

"That sounds dangerous," said Kara. "I'm not a very brave person, Danny, and I have no desire to have any more dealings with Al Price. I think this whole thing is a matter for the police to handle."

"I told you, it won't do any good," grumbled Danny. "Al Price is too smart. I won't go to the police unless I can get something on him." He hesitated a moment, then said resolutely, "It's getting late, Kara. Would you please drive me home now?"

21

"*C*arrie, would you like more hot chocolate?" Kara asked as she poured herself a second cup.

"No, no thanks," Carrie replied absently. She turned the stoneware mug slowly in her hands, her eyes downcast, her lips moving slightly, as if she were arguing silently with herself.

"I'm sorry I had to be the one to tell you about Danny," said Kara.

"No, I'm glad you did. It's just such a shock—" Carrie looked up, her eyes glinting with unshed tears. "I knew something was wrong with Danny, but I just didn't know what." She shook her head with a slow, perplexed heaviness. "But I never would have guessed drugs. I can't imagine Danny callously selling—" Her words faltered.

"He wants to get out of it," said Kara. "He wants to stop Al Price, but he doesn't know how."

"He should leave that to the police."

"That's what I told him, but he won't let it go at that."

"He'll have to," insisted Carrie. "Once I've told my father about this—"

"Then you plan to tell Wilson?"

"Yes. Tonight. He'll know what to do."

Kara sat back against the couch, her shoulders rounding in a gesture of relief. "I feel better already. I knew asking you to come over was the right thing to do. I'm glad I told you."

Carrie stood up and set her mug on the table. "I'd better

get back home now, Kara. It's not going to be easy facing my father with this news."

Kara stood up too. "I'll get your coat." She paused and gazed intently at Carrie. "Do you want me to come with you? I will, if you think it'll help."

"No, I'd better do this alone. It'll be such a blow to Dad. He's worked so hard on his drug abuse series for the paper. He hates pushers—" Carrie looked away. "And now Danny. How could he!"

Kara slipped a comforting arm around Carrie's shoulder as they walked to the door. "If it's any consolation, Danny is miserable about what he's done. He told me—"

Her words were interrupted by the shrill ring of the telephone. "Just a minute," she told Carrie as she picked up the receiver. She listened for a moment, her brow creasing, then said sharply, "Danny, what are you talking about?"

Carrie looked up in surprise. "Danny?"

Kara put her hand over the mouthpiece. "He's at the Hilltop House—Al Price's place. He says he has a plan to trap Al."

"Tell him to leave Al alone!" exclaimed Carrie. "He could get hurt."

"Danny, don't do anything foolish, do you hear me?" said Kara. "All right, all right. I'll come pick you up, but stay away from Al . . . Danny, no, you can't. Please leave it to the police. Danny—!"

Kara stared at Carrie in disbelief. "He hung up."

"What did he say?"

"He's looking for Al Price's address book."

"Address book?"

Kara nodded. "It's supposed to contain incriminating evidence in some sort of code."

"Couldn't you talk him out of it?"

"No," said Kara, grabbing her coat from the closet. "He

wants me to meet him at the back entrance of the Hilltop House in fifteen minutes. Let's go!"

The two girls rushed out the door into the crisp, early December air, pulling their coats on as they ran to Kara's car.

"I just pray we get there before Danny does anything crazy," cried Carrie as Kara's Ford merged unceremoniously with the slow-moving evening traffic.

"We'll never make it at this pace," Kara complained. She stepped on the gas and changed lanes. "We'll try the side streets. Maybe they won't be so busy."

Fifteen minutes later she turned into the winding driveway of the posh Hilltop House. The restaurant, resembling a large English Tudor-style house, sat on an incline, its parking area already filling with the dinner-hour traffic.

"Danny's nowhere in sight," groaned Carrie, looking around frantically as Kara pulled to a stop beside the back entrance.

"I'm going inside," said Kara. "Keep the engine running."

"Kara, are you sure—?"

Carrie's anxious words were swallowed by the wind as Kara strode quickly toward the back door of the restaurant. She entered the building and turned left, following the narrow hallway to Al Price's office. Surely this was the right way. She had been here for a job interview—just last summer. Shortly she spotted the door with Al's name in large black letters. Hesitating, she wondered, Could Danny be inside looking for Al's book? Or was Al Price inside? Should she knock, or walk right in, or look elsewhere for Danny?

Before she could decide, a deep male voice speaking her name made her whirl around in terror. Al Price stared suspiciously at her. "What are you doing here, duchess?" he demanded.

She gazed dumbly at him. An absurdly irrelevant thought struck her: Even in the dead of winter Al was wearing one of his macho, open-chested shirts and his flashy gold pendant.

"Were you looking for me?" he pressed on, eyeing her with a cold, quizzical incisiveness.

"I—I wondered if you were in your office," she managed in a small, quavering voice.

"I'm on my way there," he replied, taking her arm with a boldness that made her flinch. "I'm always glad for a little company, especially someone like you."

Kara pulled away with a placating smile. "I really can't stay, Al. I—"

At that moment Al's office door opened and Danny emerged. Spotting Al, the boy's face blanched. He stopped in his tracks like a cornered animal. Al stared back, first in astonishment, then with dawning comprehension as Danny fumbled to conceal the book in his hands. "You lousy punk kid!" Al growled, lunging toward him.

"Run, Danny!" Kara shouted. With a desperate surge she pushed Al off balance, then raced down the hallway after Danny. Al sprinted after them, shouting obscenities. They bounded out the door, Danny several feet ahead. He leaped into the backseat of the waiting automobile, just as Al seized Kara in a breath-stopping stranglehold.

"Get out of that car, Danny," commanded Al, "or this girl's dead!"

Kara struggled violently, reaching back in a frenzy to hit at Al's head and chest. Suddenly her fingers clasped his pendant. With a swift wrenching motion, she twisted the chain until Al began to choke. For an instant he lessened his grip. As the chain snapped, Kara darted from Al's grasp. "Move over, Carrie!" she shouted as she jumped into the driver's seat, still clutching the pendant. She pushed the accelerator all the way to the floor as Al sprang furiously for the car door, and missed.

As her Ford squealed out of the parking lot, Kara caught

a glimpse of Al in her rearview mirror. He was racing toward his own vehicle. "He's coming after us!" she gasped.

"I have his book," said Danny triumphantly. "The guys were right. It was in his desk—a secret compartment."

"You shouldn't have done it, Danny," Carrie scolded from the front seat. "You scared us half to death."

"It's not over yet," Kara announced. "Al's playing for keeps. He's just two cars behind us."

"Can't you lose him?" cried Carrie.

"I'm trying," said Kara shrilly. "I'm weaving in and out of traffic like a maniac."

"You're making some drivers mad as hornets," said Danny, looking back, as one horn sounded, then another.

Kara glanced over at the sideview mirror. Her heart plunged to her stomach. "Al's only one car behind us now!" She swerved into the next lane, barely missing a red Buick. "I have to get out of this traffic," she said urgently.

At the first opportunity she veered off onto a two-lane highway. She picked up speed, hoping against hope that Al Price hadn't seen her turn off.

But, moments later, as headlights glared disquietingly in her rearview mirror, Kara knew her worst fears were realized. Al's powerful vehicle was bearing down with frightening speed on her own straining, overheated car. He was gaining—overtaking her!

Without warning, he pulled ahead into the lane beside Kara and, in a brutal, vindictive gesture, began to edge her car off the pavement. With a jarring, grinding motion, his tires sang menacingly against her own, propelling her vehicle toward the gravel shoulder overlooking a steep ditch.

"He's going to kill us!" screamed Carrie.

Kara grappled frantically with the steering wheel, but with each vicious assault by Al's car, her vehicle vibrated convulsively toward the abutment. Then, as her Ford careened off the shoulder into darkness, Kara caught a glimpse of an oncoming car in Al's lane. Al Price's car was the bull's-eye!

22

*T*he sudden shudder and splinter of metal colliding with earth . . . the macabre shriek of humanity enmeshed in the accordion-grip of a collapsed automobile . . . then, out of a black nightmare sleep, pinpoints of sound, of sirens and groanings, of static and mechanical voices buzzing from a police radio, of shouts dissolving in dank, bone-cold air. There was pain—throbbing, pervasive. Then, nothing.

Groggily Kara rubbed her eyes, forcing open heavy, reluctant lids. The cobwebs were slowly clearing from her mind. Awareness came in sluggish, disjointed thoughts. She had been through this before—waking in a strange, sterile-white room, her body sore, the fragments of a nightmare debilitating her senses. Last time it was the fire. This time—

She stirred slightly. Pain coursed through her muscles. Her lips were dry, stiff; her head ached. "Water," she murmured, looking to one side. Her gaze settled on Greg sitting in a chair next to her bed, nearly asleep. Hearing her voice, he sprang to his feet and approached her, his eyes probing hers intently.

"Kara, you're awake, finally."

"W—What are you doing here?" she murmured.

"I've been here since last night, keeping an eye on you and Carrie." Gently he placed the straw from a plastic tumbler between her lips. "Here, take a sip."

She drank haltingly. "Last night?" she echoed in disbelief. "What time is it now?"

"Nearly dinnertime."

Kara shook her head ponderously. "There was an accident. Al Price forced us off the road. I remember Carrie screaming." She paused and stared beseechingly at Greg. "Carrie—where is Carrie?"

"In another room. Her folks are with her."

"And—Danny?"

"He's fine. A few cuts and abrasions. Nothing serious."

"Thank God!" Kara made an effort to raise herself up, then sank back dizzily on the bed. "What's wrong with me, Greg?"

"A slight concussion, but you'll be good as new after a little rest."

"When can I go home?"

"In a day or two. The doctors want to keep you under observation. They say that's routine procedure."

"I want to see Carrie," she said emphatically.

An expression of distress crossed Greg's face, fleeting but unmistakable.

"What is it?" demanded Kara. "Carrie is all right, isn't she?"

"I think she will be," replied Greg evasively.

Kara sat up shakily, her voice tremulous. "What's wrong with her, Greg? Tell me the truth."

"Please, Kara, you've got to stay quiet," he said, placing his hands paternally on her shoulders and guiding her back down.

She lay back obediently but managed a firm, "Tell me, Greg."

His shoulders sank with pained resignation. "Carrie was thrown through the windshield," he told her, his tone deep and pungent. "She has a—a head injury."

"Is it serious?"

"Yes."

"Will she . . . recover?"

"We're all praying that she will."

Tears welled in Kara's eyes. "It's all my fault," she cried. "I hurt everyone I touch—just like Anna!"

"That's not true, Kara. In fact, you and Carrie and Danny are responsible for instigating the largest investigation into the drug racket this city has ever known."

"What about . . . Al Price?" she asked.

"He was struck head on, Kara. He didn't make it," replied Greg soberly. "The police found drugs in his car—a large supply of cocaine and PCP."

Kara looked away, momentarily silent. Finally she asked, "What about Al's address book?"

"The police are studying it, but so far they haven't been able to break the code."

"Then they won't be able to arrest the ringleaders Al worked with." Kara's voice rose in alarm. "The drug traffic will continue just as before—"

Greg took her hand comfortingly in his. "A beginning has been made, Kara. That's something to be thankful for."

"What will happen to Danny?"

"He'll have to appear in juvenile court, but for now he's being released into his parents' custody. He's cooperating in the investigation. That should count for something."

Kara turned her gaze reflectively toward the wall. "It's going to be so hard for Wilson to write his last editorial on drug abuse, knowing Danny was involved."

Greg stood up and stretched his legs. "I'm afraid all Will can think of at the moment is Carrie."

"I'd like to see Will, Greg," said Kara, looking up earnestly. "Would you ask him to come by my room sometime? Maybe I could say something to help."

Greg's face clouded. "I don't think anything will persuade Will to leave Carrie's room, but I'll ask him." He leaned over and kissed her gently on the forehead. "I'd better go now and let you get some rest. But I'll be back later, okay?"

Kara smiled weakly. "That's a deal."

———

Three days later, Kara was released from the hospital. Just as she put the finishing touches on her makeup, Greg arrived to take her home. "I must say you look wonderful," he told her approvingly.

"I hope I look better than I feel," she said, turning away from the mirror to face him. "I'm still pretty wobbly."

"Well, I just happen to have an arm that's perfect for supporting wobbly young ladies." He helped her into a wheelchair the nurse had brought. "You rest a minute. Meanwhile, is there anything I can do to help?"

"I just have a few things in the closet, mainly the clothes I was wearing the night of the accident."

"I'll get them," said Greg, going to the closet. Conversationally he added, "Did Will ever get by to see you?"

"Just for a few minutes yesterday. He didn't say much. He was terribly upset about Danny and Carrie, especially Carrie. He said if she dies he wants to die too. She's not going to die, is she, Greg?"

"No, Kara. She has to get well."

"Well, I couldn't say anything to help Wilson." She stared glumly at her hands. "He's my own father, Greg, but he doesn't want my comfort."

"I'm sorry, Kara."

"Me too. At least Lynn came by this morning. We prayed together. She feels Carrie is beginning to respond."

"We'll have to find out when they'll let us visit her," said Greg.

"I doubt if we can until she's out of intensive care."

He nodded and slipped Kara's coat around her shoulders. She eased gingerly into the garment. "The accident sure made a mess of my good winter jacket," she noted. "It's all grimy and torn."

"It won't matter when you get out in that cold wind."

"I should have a scarf here somewhere," said Kara, fishing in her pocket. She looked down in surprise. "What's this?"

"What?"

Baffled, Kara held up a gleaming pendant; then, with a muffled cry, she dropped it on the floor. "It's Al's!" she exclaimed. "He always wore it."

Greg stooped down to retrieve the medallion. "How did you get it?" he asked.

"Al—he caught me. I struggled. I twisted the chain. It broke in my hand. I must have put it in my pocket without thinking when we made our escape from the restaurant."

"The pendant broke just now when you dropped it," said Greg, standing up and placing it in her hand.

"No," said Kara, "it's not broken. It's a locket. Look at what's inside. It's some sort of key."

Greg took the small metal object and turned it carefully between his fingers. "It looks like a key to a safe-deposit box, if you ask me."

Kara brightened. "Do you suppose it could lead to more evidence?"

"Could be. It must be important if this Price guy wore it all the time. I'll drop it by the police station after I take you home."

"Call me if you find out anything, anything at all," instructed Kara.

———

Greg telephoned her at ten the next morning. "Hope I didn't wake you," he said pleasantly.

"No. I got up at nine. I'm just finishing some hot chocolate and toast."

"I have good news for you," Greg continued, scarcely hiding the excitement in his voice.

"What? Tell me!"

"The key does belong to a safe-deposit box," he replied. "The police opened it and found the information they'll need to decipher the coded address book. They should have enough evidence to arrest nearly every drug racketeer in Claremont."

"That's wonderful!"

"This should be the biggest shakedown our city has ever seen, thanks to you, Kara."

"No, don't thank me. I got involved in this whole thing completely by accident—"

"Not by accident, Kara; by design. I believe the Lord had a hand in it."

Kara laughed good-naturedly. "I'm glad He knew what was going on, because I sure didn't."

"I'm going to tell Will about these latest developments," Greg said. "Also, I checked and we can see Carrie next Tuesday. I'll pick you up about four, okay?"

———

On Tuesday afternoon, when Kara and Greg entered Carrie's room, she smiled wanly at them and made a feeble joke about the bandages on her head. "I must look like King Tut," she mumbled.

"You'll be yourself in no time," Kara assured her. "I'm just so sorry this happened to you. I blame myself for getting you involved."

"Don't say that, Kara." Carrie spoke with effort. "I'm just glad that you and Danny are all right."

"We can't stay long," interjected Greg. "You need your rest, Carrie, but we'll be back tomorrow."

"Thank you," she sighed, closing her eyes. "I love you both."

"We love you too," said Kara, gently squeezing Carrie's hand.

Kara and Greg left quietly, their expressions solemn. Neither spoke until Greg swung his car out of the hospital parking lot.

"She will be all right, won't she, Greg?"

"The doctors say so."

"But she looks so weak and helpless," protested Kara. "She's always been so bubbly and full of life."

"She will be again. Believe me." Greg reached over and took her hand. "You know what we both need? A change of scene. A nice dinner out, with candlelight and music."

"Not the Hilltop House!"

"No, but some place nice just the same. What do you say?"

"I'd like that very much."

Greg drove to the Fireside Cove, an attractive steak house on the outskirts of Claremont. As a waitress showed them their table, Greg said confidentially, "This place has the best steak and lobster around."

"Can you afford that on a teacher's salary?" Kara whispered back cautiously.

"This is a special occasion," he told her as they sat down.

"What occasion?"

"An evening to forget the bad times you've had and to concentrate only on pleasant things."

She laughed ruefully. "I don't think anything can make me forget all that's happened lately."

"I'd like to try."

Kara caught a rare, warm glint in Greg's eyes, an expression almost of promise—elusive, mystifying. She smiled in spite of herself.

Greg ordered broiled filet mignon, medium rare, and lobster on the half shell, with stuffed mushrooms and baked potatoes.

"I feel positively wicked gorging myself like this," mused

Kara shortly, as she dipped her last morsel of lobster into melted butter.

"For penance, I'll brown-bag it the rest of the month," noted Greg with a boyish grin.

Later, as they left the restaurant, he said, "It's still early. Would you like to go for a drive?"

"I don't think so, Greg," replied Kara. "I'm really tired."

Obligingly he drove her home and walked her to her door. "Would you mind if I came in a minute?" he questioned as she turned the key in the lock. "I'd like to talk to you."

"No, I don't mind," she answered, going in and flicking on the light switch. "I still feel a little jittery entering an empty apartment."

"It's a nice place," he said, glancing around.

"Thanks. You should have seen the old place. Straight out of Charles Dickens, complete with rats." She laughed. "On second thought, I'm glad you didn't see it." She took his coat and nodded toward the sofa. "Sit down, Greg. I'd offer you some coffee or a soft drink, but I haven't done much shopping since coming home from the hospital."

"If you need anything, I'd be glad to go get it for you," he offered.

Kara sat down beside him and smiled appreciatively. "Thanks, Greg, but after that scrumptious dinner, I may never eat again."

"I just hope it cheered you up a little."

"It did. My spirits have definitely lifted several notches."

Greg sat forward slightly and cracked his knuckles, apparently absorbed in thought.

"What is it, Greg? You said you wanted to talk to me."

He nodded, gazing contemplatively at his hands. "I don't know if this is the time or place—" He looked up intently at her. "When I heard about the accident and realized how close I had come to losing you, it really made me stop and think. I thought about all the things we've shared the last few months—our faith in Christ, our love of literature, our special talks at the restaurant, the fun we've had just being together."

Kara stared dubiously at him. "What are you saying, Greg?"

He turned to her and in a slow, languid motion touched her face and hair with his fingertips. Gently he traced her lips, the curve of her chin. "Kara, for so long I've wanted to tell you—"

She pulled back skittishly from his touch.

"I love you, Kara."

"Greg, no—" she said, wavering.

He reached over and gathered her tenderly into his arms and kissed her. Kara's protests melted as she felt herself responding to his warmth, his touch. She knew instinctively she was where she had always belonged.

"You love me too," he whispered. "I know it. I want you, Kara. I want to marry you."

Kara stirred, forcing her mind to react against the mesmerizing balm of Greg's closeness. "No," she said, disengaging herself from his embrace. She stood up, trembling. "There can't be anything between us, Greg. You should know that."

He stood up and clasped her arm. "Please, Kara, don't turn away from me. I love you. I believe you love me."

"I can't," she insisted, fighting back tears.

"Why not?"

"I—I can't tell you."

"You're not making any sense. Why can't you love me?"

"You must know. I can't believe you don't know."

"Know what? Kara, you're talking in riddles."

She shook her head adamantly. "I simply can't love you, Greg."

"Kara, you've got to be honest with me," said Greg seriously. "This is too important for hedging."

"All right. It's . . . Carrie."

"Carrie?"

"You—you belong to her."

Greg's brows arched in consternation. "What does Carrie have to do with this?"

"Everything," cried Kara. "She loves you, Greg. She always has."

"Loves me? Kara, she's like a sister to me. There's never been anything romantic between us."

Kara crossed the room, putting distance between Greg and herself. She chose her words carefully. "Maybe there's nothing between you now, but that doesn't rule out someday. Don't you see, Greg? I can't come between you two, not if there's any chance at all for you to be together."

Greg approached her, his hand extended beseechingly. "It's you I love, Kara, only you. I want you to be my wife . . . the mother of my children. I could never feel that way about Carrie."

Kara felt herself weakening. More than anything in the world she wanted to fling herself into Greg's arms and pledge her eternal love. But no. She steeled herself against her own seething emotions. "It doesn't matter what you say, Greg," she said levelly. "In my mind you belong to Carrie, and I won't do anything to hurt her."

Greg studied her silently, his eyes dark and inscrutable as smoke, the tendons of his jaw moving almost imperceptibly. He looked as if he had been struck a terrible blow, and she winced inside, knowing she had delivered it.

Finally his expression softened. "I've never led Carrie on, Kara," he told her quietly. "We've never been anything but friends. Carrie would be the first to tell you that." He ran his hand unconsciously through his hair. "Would you want Carrie to spend her life with a man who didn't love her? Would you wish that on her?"

Kara brushed at her eyes and looked away. "All I know is that Carrie loves you with all her heart. Now, since the accident, she's more vulnerable than ever. I won't be the one to come between you. So there's nothing more to say."

"It doesn't end here, Kara," Greg said forcefully. "I won't give up on you. Your kiss told me what you refuse to admit. We belong together. I believe God wants us together."

Kara went to the closet and removed Greg's coat. "Please go now," she said. "I'm really very tired."

At the door he glanced back and smiled infectiously. "Good-night, my lovely Kara. I'll see you tomorrow."

"Good-night, Greg," she said, her voice strained.

When he had gone, she shut the door quickly and locked it, weak with a mixture of relief and remorse. She pressed her face against the door and held her fist against her mouth to muffle the convulsive sobs.

23

$\mathcal{B}$y noon the next day Kara had packed all her belongings in two supermarket packing cartons that still smelled fragrantly of laundry detergent. After a simple lunch of leftovers, she defrosted the refrigerator, cleaned the stove, scoured the floors, and gave her few remaining groceries to the elderly lady next door.

Although she worked with a grueling single-mindedness, Kara could not shake off a sensation of bitter cold. It was as if the chilly December dampness had settled upon her with a devious concentration. She could not get warm, could not stop the persistent trembling inside her. Recalling last night—the warmth of Greg's touch, his kiss—only turned the cold to pain.

She would not be warm again until she had escaped the people whose hopes and hurts and needs had fused so completely—and now clashed so overwhelmingly—with her own dreams and desires. As callous as it seemed, surgery—incisive emotional surgery, a severing of all ties—was necessary. Kara would not see Greg again; he was Carrie's. She would not see her father, Wilson Seyers, whose awkward restraint evoked an ache of emptiness she refused to endure any longer.

She would go home where she belonged, back to Westchester, to Anna. Somehow she would make a home for the two of them, pick up the pieces of their lives, or cast out the broken pieces, and start from scratch. At least this time she was not going home empty-hearted. She had Christ within her, and however new and fragile and untried that relationship might be, a small, sweet certainty prevailed: She was His, and He was hers.

Late that afternoon Kara telephoned for a taxi and rode to the hospital for one last visit with Carrie. She arrived just before visiting hours began, hoping to avoid an unexpected encounter with Greg. He would still be at school, probably wondering why she had missed class today.

Carrie's expression was more animated, her coloring not so wan. "I'm feeling better," she assured Kara. "I may even go home next week."

"Says who?" Kara challenged gently. "You or the doctor?"

"Mostly me," admitted Carrie. "I'm tired of this place already."

"That's a good sign," said Kara, sitting down. "I'm afraid I can't stay long," she added, trying to sound casual. "I—I'll be going out of town for a while."

"Out of town? Where?"

"Home to Westchester." Kara looked down at her hands. As she spoke she worked unconsciously with the cuticle of one fingernail. "With all that's happened lately I need to get away, spend some time alone. And, of course, I should see Anna again. I've neglected her for too long."

"When will you be leaving?"

"Tonight maybe . . . or tomorrow morning. I still have to see Aunt Kate before I go." Kara inspected her nail. She had pushed the cuticle back too far. Her finger began to throb.

"How will you go . . . with your car wrecked?"

"I'll take the bus, bumps and all," quipped Kara.

"But you'll miss your classes."

"Well, Christmas vacation is coming up, you know, so I'll have a few weeks off."

"I'll miss you terribly," said Carrie.

Kara forced a smile. "It's not as if you'll be alone. You

have your folks . . . and Greg. He'll keep you company while I'm gone."

Carrie nodded wistfully. "I don't know what I'd do without him, Kara. He's been so good. Mom and Dad told me how he's been here at the hospital, even when I couldn't have visitors."

"About Greg—" Kara broached the subject cautiously. "I suppose you still feel the same way about him?"

Carrie gazed dreamily at the ceiling. "I love him more every day, Kara. And I think maybe he's beginning to love me."

Kara stood up with an abruptness that nearly toppled her chair. "I must go now," she said, offering a brief kiss on Carrie's forehead. "I have just one favor to ask. Please don't tell anyone where I've gone."

"But why—?"

"I can't explain it right now, Carrie, but it's important to me."

Carrie reached out and clasped Kara's hand. "Please, sis, don't stay away too long. We all need you here."

Kara said goodbye and left quickly before the tears came. From the hospital lobby she telephoned Aunt Kate and briefly explained that she was going home to Westchester. "I'd like to see you before I go," she added hesitantly.

"I'd like to see you too, Kara. Why don't you come spend the night here," Kate suggested, "and get a fresh start in the morning."

"I was hoping you'd say that," said Kara, pleased.

As dusk settled, Kara caught a taxi back to her apartment and had the driver load her belongings while she paid the landlord an extra month's rent, since she hadn't given advance notice. She forced herself not to look back as the cab passed Claremont's city limits and headed toward Aunt Kate's home.

Catherine had hot roast-beef sandwiches ready to serve

when Kara arrived. The savory aroma and the cheery warmth of the kitchen stirred Kara's memories. The recollections were vague, an indefinable mixture of feelings and impressions, but unmistakably pleasant. "I feel as if I've sat in this kitchen before, long ago, eating hot roast-beef sandwiches," she mused.

"You have," said Kate, smiling, "when you visited here as a child. Roast-beef sandwiches were your favorite."

"They still are."

Kate set the steaming sandwiches on the table, poured two cups of hot apple cider, and sat down. "I'm sorry we haven't been in touch lately," she told Kara. "I was in Westchester visiting Anna and returned just two days ago. Yesterday I started going through my stack of newspapers and I was shocked when I read what you and the Seyers family have gone through. I called your old apartment, but they said you had moved."

"I should have called you weeks ago," said Kara apologetically. "I've been wanting to share something with you for quite a while now." She gave Kate a tentative smile. "I—I've become a Christian."

Kate's expression of surprise broadened into a luminous smile; her eyes glistened. "Oh, Kara, dear, you don't know how I've prayed for this day!"

As they ate, Kara shared with Kate the experiences that had led to her conversion. "For weeks now I've wanted to tell you I no longer have bitter feelings toward you, Kate," Kara concluded. "I suppose I'll always think of Anna as my mother, but I want you to be my friend. Will you forgive me for hurting you?"

Kate reached across the table to touch Kara's hand. Her voice trembled slightly as she said, "Where there is genuine love, there is already forgiveness. You have always owned my loyalty and my love."

"There's so much in our lives for us to catch up on," said

Kara eagerly. "I don't know where to begin—"

"We'll find the way," said Catherine. She looked carefully at Kara. "What about Wilson? How do you feel now about him?"

Kara sighed deeply. "I don't plan to see him again, Kate. I've come to realize that Ben Strickland was my father in every way that matters."

"Ben loved you very much," said Kate quietly.

"And I'll always love him," reflected Kara.

"There's something you should know, Kara," said Kate after a moment. "While I was in Westchester I told Anna that you know the truth about your background. It was time she knew. She couldn't understand why you didn't come to see her. I explained that you had a lot of things to work out in your mind right now."

"What did she say?"

"She was upset, but I assured her that in the long run it's best for everyone that you know the truth. I reminded her that she was free of the burden of keeping the secret and that now you two can build an even stronger relationship, built wholly on truth."

"Did she accept what you said?"

"I think so—eventually. You see, Anna and I have found a new closeness that we haven't known since childhood. Things aren't perfect, of course. Anna still has times when she's moody and withdrawn, when nothing anyone says can reach her."

Kara sipped her hot cider. "I hope I can help Anna. I'm going home tomorrow to tell her it doesn't matter about my past," she said, replacing her cup. "God is teaching me a great deal about forgiveness. I've given Him my bitter feelings about the fire—I blamed Anna, you know—and about the deception over my parentage. That's the wrong word; not deception, something else. I know now you and Anna and Ben were trying to protect me."

"You'll be the best medicine Anna could have," said Kate.

"Tell me, how is she?"

"She's improving steadily. I think she'll be ready to go home soon."

"Home? Where?"

"I've thought seriously about bringing her here when she's well enough to leave Westchester, but I wanted to talk with you first."

"I see," said Kara reflectively, "but I've decided I want to make a home for Anna myself. I want to take care of her."

"Then you're not planning to return to Claremont?"

"No. I feel that my life now is with Anna in Westchester."

"It won't be easy," noted Kate. "Anna will need special care for many months to come."

"I'll manage," said Kara with conviction.

Kate eyed her curiously. "You're not running away from something here in Claremont, are you, Kara?"

Kara looked down evasively at her plate. "What could I possibly be running away from?"

"Your father?"

"No, it's not him."

Kate hesitated, then said kindly, "Well, when you're ready, perhaps you'll tell me."

When they finished eating, Kara helped Catherine clear the table. Then they stood together at the sink, talking companionably as they washed and dried the dishes.

"You know, Kara," said Kate, putting away the silverware, "when I think of how you helped to uncover that terrible drug organization that had infiltrated our city, I literally get weak in the knees. I just want you to know how proud I am—of what you did."

Kara shook her head slowly. "Kate, I did very little. I stumbled into the whole mess and, thank God, I stumbled out of it intact. The Lord knows I'm not brave. I have nightmares thinking of how close Carrie came to losing her life."

Kate smiled sympathetically. "I appreciate your candor, Kara, but please don't begrudge me a little pride . . . in my daughter."

"I won't, Kate," said Kara warmly. Her tone sobered as she added, "I only pray that I can be brave now for Anna. I hope she'll forgive me for being so selfish, for turning my back on her when she needed me. Somehow I have to make it up to her."

"Would you like some company?"

"What do you mean?"

"I mean, if you like, I'll go with you. I'll drive you to Westchester tomorrow morning."

"You don't have to do that for me, Kate. This is something I should do on my own."

"You will," Catherine assured her. "But please let me go with you. I'd like to be there. I want to see the look on Anna's face when she learns her daughter has come home to stay."

24

$\mathcal{T}$he Westchester hospital lobby was decorated with strings of colored Christmas lights, and a silver-flocked tree stood beside the admittance desk. The festive atmosphere took Kara by surprise. So much had happened lately that she hadn't given much thought to the holidays. This year the season would be special—she wanted it to be special—because she would be celebrating her Savior's birthday.

Kate touched Kara's arm, breaking into her thoughts, and said, "Anna's in the convalescent wing now."

They rode the elevator to the second floor and turned right. As they entered room 6B, Kara was struck by its homey attractiveness, so different from the stark, foul atmosphere of the burn ward. She approached Anna's bed, her pulse quickening as their eyes met.

"Hello, Anna," she said.

"Oh, Kara, I've missed you!"

They embraced awkwardly. Then, sitting down on the bed, Kara gazed appraisingly at Anna. "You're looking very well. You've gained some weight, haven't you? And you're wearing such a pretty gown."

"Kate bought it for me," said Anna with the hint of a smile. "She bought me a robe and slippers too."

Kara ran her hand lightly over her mother's short, gray-brown hair. "Your hair is growing back so nicely too. I'm really pleased with how you look."

Anna reluctantly ran her fingers over the rough texture of her face. "I won't ever look the same," she said sadly. "These scars—I'll have them always."

Kara took her mother's hand and held it gently. "You look very good to me, Mother. I'm so thankful that you're alive."

"Dr. Lasky says I'm fortunate," said Anna without conviction. "For a long time I wanted to die. Sometimes I still do. But other times I want to live, even—even like this."

"I'm going to take care of you, Anna," Kara told her firmly. "When Dr. Lasky says you can be dismissed, I'm taking you home. I know you'll have to be an outpatient for a while, but I'll get us an apartment near the hospital. I'm going to be with you for as long as you need me."

Anna's eyes filled with tears. "I've needed you for so long, Kara. I didn't know if you'd ever come back to me." She glanced over at Kate. "Especially after you learned the truth." Her voice filled with a desperate intensity. "Please don't hate me for what we did. It was all for you, to protect you. We just wanted you to be happy."

Kara smiled. "I do understand, Anna. I know now that you and Ben are my parents in every way that matters."

Anna began to weep quietly. "Oh, if only Ben were still alive—"

"He'll always be alive in our hearts, Mother." Kara's voice broke slightly as she continued. "I want to ask your forgiveness, Mother, for my selfishness and anger. I was wrong to blame you for the fire and to run away from your hurt and pain. Will you forgive me?"

"Oh, Kara, there's nothing to forgive—"

"Yes, there is. From now on I want us to be open with each other, like Kate said, with no guilt or secrets between us."

Unexpectedly Anna broke into hysterical sobs. Kara sat back in surprise. "What is it? What's wrong?"

Kate approached the bed and said, "Anna, dear, do you want me to get Dr. Lasky?"

"No, no. Please, Kara, I—I have to tell you—"

"What, Mother? I'm listening."

"No. Just you. No one else."

Kate put her hand on Kara's shoulder. "I'll go down to the cafeteria for a cup of tea. That'll give you two a chance to talk alone."

"Thanks, Kate. I'll be down shortly."

As Catherine left the room, Anna struggled to compose herself. Kara handed her a tissue. "You shouldn't upset yourself like this, Mother," she said soothingly. "There's no reason now for tears. We're together. Everything's out in the open and forgiven. We have a brand-new start."

"No," said Anna, brushing agitatedly at her tears. "There's more I haven't told you."

"More?" echoed Kara. "What more could there be?"

Anna shook her head ponderously. "It's tormented me ever since that terrible night—"

"What night? You mean the fire?"

"No, not the fire." Anna stared at Kara with dark, haunted eyes. "You really don't know? You never guessed the truth?"

"What truth?" Kara demanded, perplexed.

"The truth about what happened the night your father died." The sockets around Anna's eyes seemed to deepen with dread and self-loathing. Her voice assumed a disturbing monotone. "It was my fault, Kara. I killed him. Ben's dead because of me."

A chill shot through Kara. She stood up and hugged her arms to her chest defensively. "Dad died in the crash, Anna. It was an accident. You weren't even there."

"You listen, Kara," said Anna in a low, troubled voice. "I'll tell you what happened. I'll say the words just once; then, as long as I live, I'll never say them again."

"All right, Mother," replied Kara apprehensively. "I'm listening."

"Help me up first." Anna pulled herself into a sitting position while Kara fluffed her pillows behind her. Leaning back, Anna looked at Kara with a resigned, broken expression. "I—I always loved you, Kara, you must believe that. But I also felt a seed of resentment toward you because you were Catherine's child."

Kara was puzzled. "You mean because you never had children of your own?"

"No. Because Ben loved Catherine. He married me on the rebound when Kate fell in love with Wilson Seyers. I was so in love with Ben, I was willing to marry him on any terms."

"Did he tell you he loved Kate?" questioned Kara.

"No, of course not. Not once in all our years together did he mention his feelings for her. But I knew. She was always there between us. I saw her in you. I tell you, Kara, the knowledge of Ben's love for Catherine turned my whole life sour."

"But maybe it was just your imagination," argued Kara. "Maybe you just thought he loved her."

Anna's narrow jaw stiffened. "No, I can't believe it was my imagination. It had to be true. Otherwise—"

"What, Anna? Otherwise, what?"

"Otherwise, Ben would have died for no reason."

"There was no reason," insisted Kara. "It was just one of those terrible, unforeseen accidents."

"No," said Anna dolefully. "Listen to me. The night Ben died, we were in his study arguing bitterly. I asked him why, after all these years, he had to have Catherine's picture on the wall. He said he didn't know why I had to be such a fool about Kate, and he wanted to know why I wouldn't let Kate come to visit and see her own daughter once in a while."

Anna's voice grew tenuous, faltering. "I told him he just wanted Kate to visit so he could—could see her himself."

"What did he say?" asked Kara in a half whisper.

"He denied it," replied Anna. "He said he had forgotten Catherine long ago."

"Didn't you believe him?"

"Not for a minute. I kept accusing him of loving her, of wanting Kate instead of me, even after all our years together. I wouldn't let up. I just kept after him about it."

"What—what did he do?"

Anna rubbed her frail hands together nervously. "Ben was livid with rage. I never saw him like that before. I thought he was going to explode before my eyes. But he didn't. He kept his anger inside, just barely contained. He said if I didn't believe him now, he didn't know what it would take to convince me. Do you think I would back down an inch? I told him nothing in the world would ever convince me he loved me instead of Kate."

Anna covered her eyes with her hands, as if the vision in her mind was too abhorrent to imagine.

"What happened then, Anna?" prodded Kara somberly.

"Ben didn't say another word. He stormed out of the house like a madman, slamming the door behind him. I heard him get into the car and drive away. I knew by the way his wheels screeched on the pavement that Ben was in for trouble."

"You let him go like that?" exclaimed Kara. "Why didn't you try to stop him?"

"I couldn't. He left so quickly. I guess I really didn't believe he'd go."

Kara nodded numbly. "Go on," she urged.

Anna's gaze strayed to the window. "I just sat down in a chair and waited," she said, her voice heavy, toneless. "I waited in the silence of that house for two hours before the police came to tell me the news. I knew before they said a word that I had killed Ben, that my jealousy and resentment pushed him over that cliff."

Kara stepped back instinctively, a sour revulsion rising in her throat. Then she pivoted and ran out the door, down the hall to the elevator, and out through the lobby. She burst through the double doors into the frigid early evening air. In a daze she walked down one street, then another. Escape. She had to blot out Anna's words, or they would destroy her. She ran breathlessly, her heels clicking with a staccato rhythm on the sidewalk, her eyes watering from the wind.

No, it wasn't the wind. She was sobbing with a blind, raging hysteria. There was no justice in the world, no rhyme, no reason, no sense. Her father, her beloved Ben Strickland, was dead. Why? Was it a lark in the mind of God, a cruel joke, a whim? Was God mocking her attempt at forgiveness? "Oh, God," she cried accusingly, "did you let my father die because of Anna—her terrible insecurity, her vain, destructive jealousy? It's true, isn't it! Ben is dead because of Anna!"

Loathing, worse than the trifling resentments of the past, spread through Kara like poison. Could she survive such encompassing hatred, this devastating sense of betrayal? "Why, Anna!" she demanded, her words lost in the night air. "Why did you make me hate you like this, just when I thought I had learned to forgive?"

Kara walked for what seemed like hours. She realized at last that she was in a familiar neighborhood. Her own—where she had lived with Ben and Anna, never suspecting the secrets that would ultimately destroy them. She had come here with Kate several months ago and wept when she saw the eerie remnants of her home, a charred skeleton of wood and cement. She wondered what she would find now.

Through the shadows she spotted the generous space where the house had stood. The lot was empty now. Not even the rubble remained. She walked slowly over the lawn, which, though dry and unkempt, had stubbornly survived the winter frost. The thick, untended grass covered whatever scars and blemishes might have remained on the landscape. People driving by would see no sign of the fire, in fact, no evidence that people had ever lived here. Everything was removed, smoothed over, blank, as if the house and family had never existed.

"But we do exist," Kara said aloud, shrilly. Her voice sounded absurdly small in the wide, starless expanse of sky. "It should all still be here," she cried, her voice rising with the desperation of grief, "the house, the porch, the kitchen, Dad's study, his desk and bookshelves, the pictures on the wall." She fell to her knees and dug her fingers into the hard, unrelenting earth. "They should all be right here. My father should still be here! Everything should be just as it was!"

She collapsed face down on the ground and wept, releasing all the pain and anger and frustration that had accumulated in the private recesses of her being. "Oh, God," she wailed, "I can't forgive Anna; I can't change how I feel. How can you expect me to forgive her? I can't be like you, loving and forgiving in spite of everything. It's not my nature. . . . Oh, dear Christ, your nature is supposed to be in me now. Why can't I feel it? Has my anger driven you away?"

She sat up, shivering, and pulled her coat more tightly around her. "No, you *are* here, aren't you?" she said slowly, ". . . even now, salvaging the pieces of my life. I sense it. You are bringing me back. But how . . . how can I forgive Anna?" She looked up into the impalpable darkness and said, "Oh, God, if you are really in my life, help me. I have nothing left, no one, not even myself. Please help me!"

After what seemed like hours, Kara stood up, brushed herself off, and made her way back to the hospital. She entered the lobby exhausted, numb with cold. Kate stood by the information desk, her expression anxious, pinched. When she spotted Kara, she ran, her heels clicking noisily, and embraced her with undisguised relief. "Where in the world did you go?" she cried, searching Kara's eyes. "I've been frantic, looking everywhere for you."

"I can't explain it now," Kara replied weakly. "I just had to get away for a while."

Kate touched Kara's face with concern. "You've been crying."

"I'm all right. It's just something I had to work out by myself."

Catherine managed a smile. If there's anything I can do to help—"

"No, Kate," replied Kara seriously. "God's going to have to handle this one. I just have to learn how to let Him."

"You will," said Kate. "I'm sure of it." She placed a supportive arm around Kara's shoulder as they walked to the door. "It's getting late. Instead of driving back to Claremont, let's just find the nearest motel, okay?"

"That's a terrific idea," sighed Kara. "All I want now is a hot bath and a comfortable bed to collapse into."

Kate hesitated. "Do you want to see Anna again before we go?"

Kara shook her head soberly. "Not tonight, Kate. It's too late. But tomorrow or the next day I have to talk to her about . . . forgiveness. God's—and mine. Will you help me then?"

25

Kara studied the attractive display of flowers in the hospital gift shop—lovely vases of chrysanthemums, bouquets of red and yellow roses, geraniums, and gladiolus. "I don't know what to buy for Anna," she told Kate. "What do you think?"

"How about the poinsettias, over here?" suggested Kate. "They're bright and festive, and Christmas is only a few days away."

"Great," said Kara. "I want the apartment to look just right for Anna. Cheerful, Christmasy. Maybe we should get two plants."

"No, dear," said Kate, smiling tolerantly. "You've been fussing over that apartment all week. You've got a beautiful tree, and presents, and a wreath on the door. All that's missing is the aroma of home-baked bread."

"I thought of it, but I'm a lousy cook," quipped Kara. She paused and looked uncertainly at Kate. "I'm really nervous. Do you think Anna's ready to come home?"

"Dr. Lasky says she is. Of course, she'll have to come back to the hospital every day for therapy. It's going to be a big responsibility for you, Kara. Are you ready?"

Kara nodded. "Yes, you know I have to do this, Kate, for Anna and myself."

"Well, just to remind you, I'll be only a phone call away if you need me. I'd be glad to come stay here in Westchester with Anna for as long as she's an outpatient."

"That won't be necessary . . . honest."

"Just the same, I'd feel better if I knew you were returning to college and getting your education."

Kara managed a faint smile. "I will someday. But right now Anna has to come first."

"Well, as soon as Anna can leave Westchester, I want you both to come stay with me in Claremont. The house is large enough for all of us, and it would be such a joy to have you both with me."

"We'll see," said Kara. "At the moment we have to concentrate on checking Anna out of here and taking her home."

Kate handed Kara one large poinsettia plant. "Okay, why don't you get this and take it up to Anna and see that she's ready to go, and I'll go to the office and sign the papers for her release."

"All right. I'll see you upstairs."

After paying for the plant, Kara took her time walking through the corridors to Anna's room. It hardly seemed possible that Anna was finally going home. Perhaps even more incredible, reflected Kara, was the way God had worked in her own feelings this past week. The night she had learned the truth about her father's death, she had been inundated with hatred and rage. Her feelings, starkly exposed, provided a frightening vision of rancor and viciousness she had not supposed she could possess. It had taken that evening in the motel with Aunt Kate—a time of intense prayer and anguish and finally surrender of her bitterness to God—to bring the first traces of healing. In the days since then, God had begun to give Kara His own love for Anna. Now, when remnants of resentment or self-pity surfaced, she turned immediately to God. She was discovering that only by daily emptying her heart of self could she make room for Christ to fill her with His love and power.

Still, the one feeling she hadn't quite managed to dispel was her love for Greg. She tried to assuage her aching loneliness with the reminder that Greg and Carrie would be happy together as God intended. Nevertheless, every day, in her mind's eye she traced Greg's face—his deep-set hazel eyes, his strong, angular features, his solid jaw, his half smile of amusement. In her imagination she could hear his deep, spontaneous laugh, his low and gentle voice when he spoke her name. He was woven inextricably into every thought and feeling and memory. It was a paradox: God had freed her of her bitterness, but He seemed unwilling to free her of this hapless, quixotic love.

Briskly, Kara tucked away her memories and drew her lips into a grin as she entered Anna's room. "Merry Christmas, Mother," she said, setting the poinsettia on the bedside table.

"Now why did you go and buy a plant when I'm going home?" chided Anna with a small, pleased smile.

"This is a going-home present," announced Kara. "And I see you're wearing the new dress Kate brought you. It looks lovely."

"It's a little large, and not quite the style I would have picked."

"It looks fine, Mother. Just think. This is the big day. Are you ready to go home?"

Anna grimaced slightly. "I thought I was ready months ago, but now that the day is here I'm not so sure. I feel a bit shaky."

"Well, Kate and I will help you to adjust all we can. But you have to tell us what you need." Kara looked around the room. "Are you packed?"

Anna nodded. "The nurse helped me this morning. But I don't have much to take. Everything was lost in—" Her voice broke. "Oh, Kara, if only we had our own beautiful house to go home to!"

Kara sat down on the bed and patted Anna's arm. "We aren't going to think about that, Mother. The past is behind us. We're going to think only of today."

"I'll try, Kara. I just wish I had your strength."

Kara smiled sympathetically. "I told you when we talked several days ago that it's not my strength I depend on. I couldn't have come through these past few months, or even these last few days, without God's help."

"That's nice for you, Kara," murmured Anna distractedly. "Everyone needs faith of some sort. Perhaps someday you can help me understand . . ."

"I'd be glad to try—"

A sudden knock on the door caught both Kara and Anna's attention. "Kate?" Kara began, but she gasped as her gaze focused on Greg standing in the doorway.

"Hello," he said with a spontaneous grin. "The door was open, but I thought I'd better knock anyway."

"Greg, what are you doing here?" cried Kara, barely finding her voice. She stood up and approached him with tentative steps. "You weren't supposed to know where I was."

"It didn't take a detective to figure you'd come back here, Kara."

"You shouldn't have come—"

"I would have come sooner, but I had to finish my classes before the holidays." He looked amiably at Anna and extended his hand. "You must be Kara's mother. I'm Greg Arlen."

"Greg is one of my instructors at Claremont City College," Kara explained uneasily.

"Nice to meet you, Mr. Arlen," said Anna. She looked knowingly at Kara and added, "Does Mr. Arlen take such an interest in all his students?"

"We're friends too," replied Kara. "Greg is the youth director at the church I was attending in Claremont."

Greg took Kara's elbow and said confidentially, "I talked with Dr. Lasky. He told me you're taking your mother home today."

"Yes. We're leaving as soon as my Aunt Kate gets here. She's checking Anna out."

"I'd like to have a few minutes of your time first, Kara. We need to talk."

"I can't, Greg. We have nothing to say to each other."

"Yes, we do. Please, just come down to the cafeteria with me. Surely you can take a few minutes for a cup of coffee."

"Go with him, Kara," said Anna with a flutter of her hand. "I'd just as soon rest quietly until Kate gets here."

"Are you sure, Mother?"

"Positive. Please, both of you, go and have your little visit."

"I won't be long," Kara assured her as she followed Greg to the door.

In the cafeteria, Kara sat down at a corner table while Greg got their coffee and two sweet rolls.

"This reminds me of our times together after class," he said, placing the tray on the table and sitting down.

Kara automatically stirred cream and sugar into her cup. "Please don't talk about those days, Greg."

"I'm sorry, Kara, but lately I can't think about much else. You've been in my thoughts every moment since you left Claremont."

"Greg, you're making this very hard for me," she said, sitting forward intently. "Don't you see? Your coming here can't change anything between us."

He took her hand in his. "I love you, Kara. Surely that counts for something."

"No. We each have our own lives, Greg, our separate obligations." She retrieved her hand and slowly sipped her coffee. After a moment she asked with forced brightness, "How is everyone in Claremont?"

"They're all right," replied Greg. "Danny will be going before the judge next week. We're trusting the court will take into consideration his helpfulness to the police. Danny's lawyer is going to recommend that Danny be assigned to help out on a regular basis at the local drug rehabilitation center."

"How does Danny feel about that?"

"He likes the idea. Because of his experiences, he thinks the kids may be more likely to listen to him. He's really changed, Kara. Danny's a broken, contrite boy. In fact, we've had some good talks together about the Lord."

"That's wonderful, Greg. I'm so pleased." She hesitated before asking, "And how are the Seyers?"

"Lynn and Wilson are fine. Their spirits are rising every day with Carrie's recovery." Greg gave Kara a penetrating glance. "Wilson made it a point of asking me to give you his regards. I think he does care about you."

Kara unconsciously turned the handle of her coffee cup. "He's probably just relieved to have me out of town."

"No," countered Greg. "He said to me, 'Tell Kara not to forget us.'"

Tears welled in her eyes. "Oh, Greg, I could never forget them!"

"What about me?"

"You too," she admitted reluctantly. She broke off a piece of sweet roll and ate without interest. "How is Carrie?" she questioned finally, not sounding as casual as she wished.

"I told her how I feel about you," said Greg soberly.

"Oh, Greg, you didn't!"

"I had to, Kara. I waited until she was feeling well enough, and I tried to be as kind and tactful as I could. I didn't tell her I knew about her feelings for me."

"What—what did she say?"

"Very little." He paused. "But she did give me a letter for you."

"A letter?"

"She said it was important." He removed an envelope from his coat pocket and handed it to her. Kara tore it open and quickly read the small, neat handwriting.

Dear Kara:

Greg has told me how he feels about you, and now
I understand why you left Claremont so suddenly. You
didn't want to hurt me. I appreciate your loyalty, but I
have only myself to blame for my mistaken ideas about
my future with Greg. God has been teaching me a lot
about myself these past few days. I was wrong to make
plans for my life and expect God merely to rubber
stamp them with His approval. I don't know what God
has planned for you or Greg, but please don't let my
mistake affect your feelings for him. I miss you, Kara,
and want you to return to Claremont. The whole family
does.

Your sister,
Carrie

Kara handed the letter to Greg to read and said quietly,
"I'm glad Carrie realizes there can't be anything between you.
This past week Anna taught me about the danger of marrying
someone whose love you can't be sure of. I would never wish
that experience on Carrie." She hesitated. "But that doesn't
alter my decision about us."

"Then you're saying we have no future together, regardless?"

"No. Oh, I don't know," she said, flustered. "Right now
I'm too confused to know how I feel."

Greg ran his hand lightly over Kara's arm. "If you can
look me in the eye and tell me you don't love me, I'll go away
and never brother you again."

Kara shook her head miserably. "Oh, Greg, don't you
understand? It doesn't matter how I feel. I couldn't leave
Anna now. She needs me."

"But you have your own life to live, too, Kara." He
sighed deeply and shook his head. "I'm not asking you to turn

your back on your responsibilities. These are things we could work out together."

Kara pushed back her chair and stood up. "I'd better get back upstairs, Greg. Anna and Kate are waiting for me."

Greg stood up too. "All right. Let's go."

As they walked together through the lobby, "White Christmas" wafted from the overhead speakers. Miniature lights blinked on the walls like tiny stars. At the elevator Greg took Kara's hands in his and said seriously, "Goodbye, my dear Kara."

She stared up at him. "Aren't you coming back upstairs?"

"No, I'm heading back to Claremont."

"So soon?"

"You've made it clear there's no reason for me to stay."

She searched his eyes. "You will . . . write sometime?"

He smiled grimly. "No, Kara, I won't. But if you ever decide you can say those words—I love you, Greg—then you call me." He leaned over and kissed her cheek fondly, then turned and walked away.

She stood numb, immobilized, watching as he crossed the red- and green-spangled lobby to the wide double doors. As he reached for the door, she shouted urgently, "Greg, wait!"

He pivoted and looked her way.

"Don't go!" she pleaded, running across the lobby toward him. He ran too, caught her joyously in his arms, and swung her around until her feet left the floor.

"Oh, Greg, I love you, I do love you," she cried, laughing and weeping at once.

He embraced her, kissing her lips, her hair, her eyes, her tears. "My lovely, dearest Kara," he said ardently. He circled her waist with his arm and, together, their gaze locked raptly, they walked toward the elevator in perfect step.